Written according to the new syllabus of **T. Y. B. A. Paper IV Special English** of Pune University. Also useful for other universities and M. A. & SET-NET Exam. in English.

Basics of Literary Criticism

Dr. Vilas Salunke

Diamond Publications

Basics of Literary Criticism

Dr. Vilas Salunke

First Edition : August 2010

ISBN : 978-81-8483-320-1

© **Diamond Publications**

Cover Design :
Sham Bhalekar

Published by :
Diamond Publications
264/3 Shaniwar Peth, 302 Anugrah Apartment
Near Omkareshwar Temple, Pune - 411 030
☎ 020-24452387, 24466642

info@diamondbookspune.com
www.diamondbookspune.com

Sole Distributor :
Diamond Book Depot
661 Narayan Peth
Appa Balwant Chowk, Pune 411030
Tel. - 24480677, 66020282

Preface

It gives me great pleasure to present *Basics of Literary Criticism* primarily to the students who are doing their graduation with English Special. Literary Criticism is an important part of English major courses in most of the Universities in India. In fact, this subject continues at post graduate level and later on forms a part of the course work to be completed at the level of NET/ SET (National Eligibility Test and State Eligibility Test) in English, which is a qualifying examination for appointment as Lecturers in senior colleges. However, the student community of English special courses, in general, finds Literary Criticism a difficult subject. Unless the 'Basics of Literary Criticism' are not clear to the students, further complicated aspects of Literary Theory, particularly in Contemporary Criticism, prove quite heavy for them. This book aims at providing the essentials of English Literary Theory and Criticism for the beginners. The book, however, will be useful to students and teachers of English Literature throughout their educational career.

Basics of Literary Criticism, it may be noted, has been planned mainly as a Textbook for English Special Paper IV: Introduction to Literary Criticism and Critical Appreciation. This paper contains most of the topics that a student needs when he/she begins a specialized study of English literature for a graduate course at a special/major level in any Indian university. This needs to be treated as a TEXT BOOK because it contains original critical texts by well-known critics like Sidney, Dr. Johnson, Wordsworth, Matthew Arnold and T.S. Eliot. I have given abridged versions of these texts, editing them for the convenience of students of this course. The book, therefore, is to be used as a textbook in the class both by teachers and students of English Special. I am sure the book will serve the student community maintaining a high standard of the prescribed course.

I am grateful to Shri Dattatray Pashte, Director, Diamond Publications, Pune and the staff of his publishing house for helping me bring out the book within a short period.

Dr. Vilas Salunke
(Retd.) Reader in English

About the Author

Dr. Vilas Salunke

M.A. Ph.D.

Retired Reader in English, Post Graduate Dept of English, K.T.H.M. College, Nashik

Ph.D. on "Thematic Structure in Robert Frost," Karnatak University, Dharwad, 1982

M.Phil and Ph. D. Research Guide, University of Pune, YCM Open University, Nashik

Areas of Interest : American literature, Modern British Poetry and Drama, English Language and Linguistics, Translation Studies and Literary Theory and Criticism

Research articles published on: Robert Frost, T. S. Eliot, Edward Albee, Tennessee Williams, Wallace Stevens, Anita Desai and Jai Nimbkar.

Textbooks published : (For University of Pune) 1. Chief Editor, *The Mystic Drum: An Anthology of Poems in English*, Orient Longman, 1999

2. Co-Author, *A Spectrum of Literary Criticism*, Frank Brothers, 2001,

(For M.A. English*): Contemporary Critical Theory (I)* A.V. Publishers, 2003, *Contemporary Critical theory (II)*, 2004, *Selections from Contemporary Criticism (I)*, A. V. publishers, 2007, *Selections from Contemporary Criticism (II)*, 2008

Literary Translation from Marathi into English:

1. Kusumagraj, *Blooms of the Earth*: *Selected Poems*, Writers Workshop, Kolkata, 1999

2. G.A. Kulkarni, *A Journey Forever : Iskilaar and Other Stories*, Frog Books, Mumbai, 2010

Contents

1
Principles of Literary Criticism

(1) What is Criticism?

Literary criticism is the study, analysis, and evaluation of imaginative literature. Everyone who expresses an opinion about a book, a song, a play, or a movie is a critic, but not everyone's opinion is based upon thought, reflection, analysis, or consistently articulated principles. As people mature and acquire an education, their ability to analyze, their understanding of human beings, and their appreciation of artistic craftsmanship should increase. The study of literature is an essential component in this- growth of reflection.

Sometimes students object to analysis and ask, "Why do we have to analyze everything? Why can't we just enjoy the books we read in English?" These are good questions, and there are some good answers for them. First, talking about an experience, actual or vicarious, is one way of increasing enjoyment. Second, sometimes talking about an experience involves recreating it in words, but it can also involve the search for meaning, in short, analysis. Finally, as Socrates said, "The life which is unexamined is not worth living." Analysis, or examination, increases awareness and understanding; it is part of the maturation process. The analysis of literature has always been part of a liberal education. When a work of literature is studied without reference to history or to the life of the author, the approach is intrinsic, or formalistic. However, literature is related to two other humanistic disciplines: philosophy and history. Philosophy explores basic, general ideas, such as truth, beauty, and goodness. History attempts to ascertain what happened in the past and why it happened. Philosophy may help readers to understand the general ideas, or themes, of a literary work. History helps to elucidate the life and times of the author.

Traditionally, literary studies were conducted within the three humanistic disciplines of literature, history, and philosophy. In the twentieth century, the social sciences have been used to develop new approaches to criticism. Psychology has helped to illuminate the motivations of characters and the writers who create them. Sociology has revealed the relationships between the works the author produces and the society that consumes them. Anthropology has shown how ancient myths and rituals are alive and well in the plays, poems, and novels that are popular today.

Literary criticism has been a social institution for many centuries. Different ages take different approaches, but the activity is constant. Authors are aware of criticism so that it is probably not entirely fair to say that the literary critic reads meanings into the texts that were never intended by the author. Literary criticism is not "reading between the lines" - it is reading the lines very carefully, in a disciplined and informed manner. This is why it is possible to speak of some of the approaches discussed in this booklet as elements of literature. That is, it is valid to speak of archetypal elements in a literary text, sociological elements in a literary text, and formal elements in a literary text. The approaches to literature do not put the elements there; they are already there. The approaches help to reveal and clarify them.

Literary criticism, therefore, is the analysis of works of literature by defining, classifying and considering their genre, structure and value.

Need of Criticism

If man is god's best creation, as it is believed; we have to ask a fundamental question: what are the qualities or faculties that make him the best of all the species on the earth? The general answer given, and in which most people believe, is that man has intelligence; and being more intelligent he is the best. But the earlier discussion, about fine arts and literature as fine art, points towards a different answer to the above question.

It is the faculty of imagination that really distinguishes man from the other species in nature because it is basic to human creativity. Fine arts, of which man probably is the sole creator, are undoubtedly human achievement. Literature is the most common of fine arts shared by most people and it is therefore imperative that we have to decide the quality of literature that we read, or have to or ought to read, if we really have to enjoy literature reading. It is here that we come to the field of literary criticism because it is the study of literature and we cannot keep ourselves away from it whether we read literature in order to enjoy or study it in all its aspects in order to appreciate it fully. It is literary criticism that helps us appreciate literature fully.

Definition and Principles of Literary Criticism

If most of the readers of literature don't want to be 'critics', why do we need literary criticism at all, is a question that should be answered first to ascertain its need. Let us take some common and familiar situations. Ask anyone who has read a good book or seen a good movie, why he/she likes the book/movie. You will generally find the person fumbling for words, uncertain about what to say or giving reasons, which are totally irrelevant. Tell anyone who is a voracious reader of bestsellers to read either Ernest Hemingway's *The Old Man and the Sea* or Arundhati Roy's *God of Small Things* and then ask him/her the earlier question; you will probably get the same reaction. This clearly proves that our response to literature needs to be strengthened by insights that literary criticism can offer us, without which we will love good books but will fail to know why we love them, and what precisely are their good qualities.

Literary criticism is a journey of exploration into the nature of literature in all its forms enabling us, to begin with, to distinguish between a good book and a bad book, and then to train us through its insights to distinguish for ourselves between a good book and a great one. It helps us recognize its literary quality, opening up for us the whole world of pleasure and imaginative experience and intellectual stimulus, which we may not discover without its help.

The purpose of literary criticism is to quicken and refine our perceptiveness so that we can understand the exact nature of the pleasure we derive from what is the best in literature. A critic's task is "of easing or widening or deepening our response" to literature, as Schreiber says. We share or partake of his insights to become a critic, a judge of literature as the original Greek word 'crites' suggests. Literary criticism produces, in a way, critics who continue its function on their own, to indirectly prove the dictum, "Every man his own critic." Even if every reader is a critic in his own right, what he gives is only a personal response to literature, but we should know that a mere subjective reaction is not criticism. In fact it is literary criticism that helps every reader to become a good critic of literature- a critic whose subjective response is modified/ corrected/ sensitized/ upgraded/ strengthened by the objective standards offered him by the insights in criticism. In this sense, literary criticism continually helps a reader reach within him an amalgam of his subjective response and the objective standardized evaluation of a work of art, and this process of help or enrichment goes on till the reader himself becomes 'his own critic' in the true sense of the term. In a way, literary criticism, as a process, perpetuates itself by producing, slowly but surely, literary critics to prove the dictum, 'Everyman his own critic'.

Socrates was the first person to distinguish between the ability to criticize and the ability to compose literature. If it had suited his purpose, he might have said that power to enjoy poetry is quite different from the power to analyze it rationally. Socrates for the first time pointed out that criticism is a distinct species of literary activity and also why it is distinct. This is probably the beginning of a discussion on Literature (in fact, on all fine arts) and its enjoyment and therefore it is the beginning of literary criticism in the western world.

The realm of literature is occupied by activities of three distinct powers: the power to create, the power to enjoy and the power to criticize. The chief distinction of the power to criticize from the other two is that it can be acquired. Though criticism is an intuitive as well as conscious activity, its process appeals to certain intellectual principles that can be set out, studied and put in to practice in an orderly system. But there are no principles that will tell you how to create literature or how to enjoy it. Criticism does not pretend to account for the state of the mind in which literature is created, nor for that in which it is enjoyed. It assumes their existence. That is to say, it assumes the fact that literature exists and then it proceeds to enquire into the nature of literature and to expound it. As soon as a man becomes aware that it would suit his purpose to say something in one way and not in the other, criticism begins. In this sense, criticism begins when literature begins. Though criticism begins with vague instinctive preference, it goes on to become a distinct and conscious activity that can be rationally justified; there is always an appeal to intellectual principles in it.

However, criticism helps the creative writer as well as the reader who enjoys literature. It enables the man who has the creative power to make the most intelligent and efficient use of his creative powers. To the reader, it makes the enjoyment of literature the most intelligent and therefore the most discriminating and illuminating experience.

Criticism, as distinct from creation and enjoyment, consists in asking rational questions about literature and answering them. These are of two kinds: the first proceeds from literature in general to particular pieces of literature and the second proceeds from the particular to the general. In the first kind of enquiry, we start with the general view of literature asking the following type of questions: What is literature? What are the qualities common to all literature? What is the function of literature? The results of such an enquiry can be set out in a system of principles which express our understanding of the nature of literature. These principles are intellectual principles, but they are not laid down a *priori* as prescribing the nature which literature ought to have. The nature of literature is a fact, which exists, weather we investigate it or not. Whether we criticize it or not, literature exists on its own as an objective fact. The principles of literature offered by literary criticism, however, are the answers, which our intellect gives to us when we ask what sort of fact literature is. And this kind of enquiry may be called the theory of literature.

On the other hand, the second kind of enquiry, which proceeds from particular to general, deals with the merits of particular pieces of literature, be it a poem, a play, or a novel. This is what usually goes under the name of criticism and may be called criticism proper. The question here is not of literature in general, but of unique qualities in concrete examples of literary pieces. Criticism asks what qualities give a particular work its peculiar individuality. The mood and the spirit as well as the choice of matter and its technique, and also the use of language-these are the subjects of criticism, and its end is to assess the literary merits of a work of art. It can be said that literary criticism deals with what may in the broadest sense be called style of a work of art.

Indeed, no clear line can be dawn between theory of literature and criticism proper because both refer continually to each other. This ought to be so because criticism proper naturally prefers to stand on something more reliable than impressions, which may be based on personal likes and dislikes or even prejudices. Therefore the history of criticism has been the history of attempts to formulate views for criticism. Only the principles that express the nature and define the functions of literature in general can determine what is essential in any kind of literature; and only by appealing to what is essential can criticism provide reliable rules. Thus theory of literature and criticism proper necessarily overlap. They are mutually dependant.

Nature and Functions of Criticism

Literary criticism brings in an expert's opinion to examine a piece of literary work. The expert is a literary critic who uses his talent and training to look into merits and demerits of a work in order to pass a judgment upon it. However, criticism is not mere record of judgments. It includes the whole mass of writing that is written about literature proper. The object of criticism is analysis and/or interpretation and/or evaluation of a work of literary art, be it a poem, a play, a novel. These functions vary from critic to critic in that they combine one or more of them according to their own viewpoints. Criticism deals with poetry, drama, novel and other literary forms, which deal with life directly. If creative literature is an interpretation of life through various forms of literary expression, criticism is an interpretation of that interpretation as well as of the forms of literature. This does not mean that criticism has nothing to do with life directly. Literature is interested in life and personality is one of the chief facts of life. Criticism, which tries to interpret the personality of a great writer as it is revealed in a literary work of art, truly deals with life as literature does. We all know that a poem does not come out of a hat; it has to come from a head that is human. If a great writer makes us realize the larger sense and meaning of life, a critic makes us realize the larger sense and meaning of literature itself.

Literary criticism has two major functions to perform, one of interpretation and the other of judgment. The history of criticism shows that these two functions were combined till recent times. A majority of critics have used interpretation as a means to reach judgment which they have thought to be the real end of criticism. These two functions have been separated in modern criticism as it is maintained that the critic's duty is not judgment but only interpretation or exposition. The real aim of a critic is to penetrate the heart of a work, to separate its essential qualities of beauty and strength, to distinguish between what is temporary and what is permanent in it and to explain and examine the artistic and what is permanent in it and to explain and examine the artistic and moral principles that have guided the writer. In this sense, a critic is expected to make what is implicit in a work of art.   If the task of a writer is to conceal his art, that of a critic is to reveal it, to exhibit the interrelations of different parts to bring out the connections of each to the whole. Thus, explaining, unfolding and illuminating are the task of a critic to reveal all aspects of its content, its art and its design. After this he may evaluate it, justifying his stand. But his primary concern is to know the book and help us know it. He need not pass any definite judgment upon it based on his own taste or on any organized body of critical opinions.

It is rather difficult to reconcile the claims of Interpretation and Judgment because the two are not easily separable. G. Wilson Knight says, "Criticism is a process of deliberately objectifying works under consideration, the comparison of it with other similar works in order to show in what respect it surprises or falls short of these works." In this sense, a critic should avoid value judgment; he should not take a moral stand and become a judge. In conclusion, we can say that interpretation and judgment are complementary to each other; they are generally inseparable in practice.

(2) Fine Arts and Literature as Fine Art: Some Characteristics

From the beginning criticism has dealt with literary arts like poetry and other forms of literature and fine arts like painting, sculpture, music, dance and the like. As a branch of Aesthetics, criticism has analysed the creation of beauty in the sphere of all these arts. Let us discuss some of these to bring out the definite features along with their distinctions.

Fine Arts and Useful or Mechanical Arts

The fine arts are those which have primarily to do with imagination and taste, and are applied to the production of what is beautiful. They include poetry, music, painting, engraving, sculpture, and architecture; but the term is often confined to painting, sculpture, and architecture.

Useful arts refer to the employment of means to accomplish some desired end; or the adaptation of things in the natural world to the uses of life; or the application of knowledge or power to practical purposes. Useful are involve systematic application of knowledge or skill in effecting a desired result. It also includes an occupation or business requiring such knowledge or skill. Hence these arts are also called the mechanical arts because the hands and body are more concerned than the mind in them; as in making clothes and utensils.

Art and Craft
Craft work is skilled work: any kind of craft must involve the application of a technique. Craft involves technique but not necessarily mechanical technology. Craft implies the application of human intelligence and usually when we use the word we have in mind the application of the human hand. The craftsman has tools at command but it is human guidance not tools that accomplishes a task.

The concept of craft is historically associated with the production of useful objects at least since the 18th century. The craftsman's teapot or vase should normally be able to hold tea or flowers, while the artist's work is typically without utilitarian function. The crafts tend to produce things which are useful for various human purposes, and though they may be pretty or pleasing in any number of ways, craft objects tend to exhibit their prettiness around a purpose external to the object itself. To this extent, the crafts aren't arts, according to an idea of the great philosopher Immanuel Kant. Works of art, Kant said, are intrinsically final: they appeal purely at the level of the imagination and aren't good for any practical utility.

These two symptoms of craft, that craft involves the application of intelligent skill (often some kind of handwork), and that it commonly results in the production of useful objects, are uncontroversial, but they still don't get us very far in distinguishing craft from art. Because, of course, works of art in painting, in music and its performance, in poetry, and elsewhere normally require skill, and, moreover, many great works of art are also objects of enormous practical value, for example, works of architecture.

Literature as Fine Art: Comparison with other Fine Arts
Generally, in order to bring out the distinction between one fine art with another, the Hegelian method of grading the arts is followed. Hegel grades the fine arts in their order-assigning to architecture the lowest and to poetry the highest status. In considering the fine arts as a group, certain criteria need be observed. The criteria, which bring the

fine arts of architecture, sculpture, painting, music and poetry under one umbrella, are as follows:

1. Each and every fine art must have a material basis or medium of representation.

2. Each and every fine art must have its own range of subjects, that is, external objects from nature which become its subject in the art.

3. Each fine art employs means through which it brings the medium under the purview and cognizance of the senses and particularly the mind of the artist.

4. Each of the fine arts adopts a manner, a way in which to represent its art in such a way that the mental aspect of the artist is more prominent than the medium.

5. The merit of each fine artist in his representation of reality is conditioned by his medium. The more 'material' is the medium, the less free the artist and the less restrained or limited his art is.

Literature, and every form of it-be it poetry, drama, fiction-observes these criteria broadly. Let us, briefly, see how each of these fine arts follows the criteria, and then discuss poetry or literature which surpasses the other fine arts.

Architecture has as its medium of representation stone, which is solid, prominently material. Its subject is limited-buildings and the highest of all, places of religious worship. Here, the artist's mental aspect, his imagination and all his artistry cannot, successfully, hide or undermine its material basis. So structures, except the structure like that of a place of worship, cannot appeal to the faculties of heart, mind, and soul, appreciably.

Sculpture has stone as its material basis, but the sculptor through representing animal and human forms in their state of arrested motion creates that resemblance to reality, which can momentarily beguile the spectator, but cannot, for want of the attribute of movement appeal to the perceptions of the spectator, sufficiently.

Painting addresses itself to a two-dimensional plane surface of the canvas or other materials, which are less solid and less material. By the use of lines, colours and brush to advantage, the painter can appeal to the emotional, intellectual and even spiritual faculties of the spectator, to move him. The painter reduces the lack of the attribute of movement by representing arrested motion of objects, persons and scenes. He idealizes the real in his representation and interprets the real in his mental aspect and so he can move the spectator.

Music has 'sounds' as is medium and can represent a lyric, a song and the burden of the song, in a way that it appeals to the superior faculties. The musician can represent the sounds of objects and natural phenomenon like thunder, storm, lightning and emotional aspects like sorrow and joy The art of music cannot present forms or meaning or ideas contained in a lyric, due to the vagueness of sounds in their representation of meaning. Music however can create a good deal of effect.

Poetry, a major form of literature, is in a position to subordinate its medium to transmute it-the words- to evoke emotions, ideas through symbols, and bring up pictures through description and employing effective devices, appeal to the highest faculty of man, that is, the soul.

From the time of Plato and his disciple Aristotle all art including fine arts and literature are considered imitative. Through imitation every fine art aims at producing a resemblance to reality. Literature does this through idealizing and projecting or formulating a truth within the limits of the rules governing it.

Literature, like the other fine arts, records the impression made by external realities upon the artist. The architect gives the spectator his impression of how beautiful stones will look if arranged in a particular order and according to rules of symmetry governing that art. In architecture, a building is the architect's apprehension of beauty in real objects-stones-if represented in a particular manner. Similarly, the sculptor by imitating real human and animal forms presents a beautiful work- his sculptural piece- through his mental aspect to impress the spectator. Painting and music perform the same function. The painter represents resemblances of real objects with emotions close to real ones through colour and other materials. His aim is to impress the beholder through moving him, that is, appealing to his finer faculties. The musician, through rhythmic sounds in combination moves the listeners. The poet as a fine artist does it in a better way than all the other forms of fine arts with words, which are a powerful medium. Literature records the impressions which natural objects and human beings have made upon writers. Like all arts and fine arts literature, too, is a fine art as it appeals to the finer sensibilities of man.

In the final analysis, every piece of all old architecture, every piece of ancient sculpture, an old painting of Leonardo da Vinci, a musical composition of Beethoven and a great literary classic represent the brain and intellect and the quality of the mind of the race and the country to which the artists belonged. Literature, akin to all the other fine arts is, to use Basil Worsfold's words, the 'brain of humanity.'

Poetry and Painting

Plato was the first to point out that a common property unites all fine arts- that they are all modes of imitation. After him Aristotle laid down criteria for imitative arts. Each art is governed by a medium, an object and a manner of representation of reality, within the universal laws of beauty in order to yield pleasure.

Plutarch and Horace in the Roman world and Lessing, Croce, Ben Jonson and Sidney in his '*An Apology for Poetry*' have all agreed that there exists some resemblance between the fine arts of painting and poetry. They all accepted that "poetry is a speaking picture, and picture mute poetry." But, while resemblances can be marked, the two arts can never be equated as such, though as fine arts, they share the common criteria of medium, objects and manner of representation. Croce entirely supports the equation of painting and poetry, but Lessing rejects it by saying that "bodies with their visible properties are the peculiar subjects of painting........actions are the peculiar subjects of poetry." He goes on to argue, convincingly, that painting can represent only a single movement of time, while poetry, deals with a temporal sequence while describing objects. So with this difference between the two fine arts having come to notice, it becomes necessary that the two fine arts be viewed afresh.

Commenting on the likeness between painting and poetry, one can say that both are imitative arts, both aim at creating a semblance of reality and both tend to beguile the spectator by exploiting to the full the imaginative faculty and artistry to select, to interpret reality through the mental aspect, with the ultimate aim of pleasing the spectator. Here ends the resemblance. In many other respects the two arts are different.

The prime difference relates to the medium or material basis. Painting has a two- dimensional plane, brush, colours etc as its medium. Poetry has words in various combinations as its sole medium. 'Words' transcend dimensions and can describe multi-dimensional activities or several activities simultaneously.

But painting lacks the attribute of motion or movement. It can represent objects at a moment of time in their arrested motion. It is art in repose or at rest. It can represent space, but not continuous or successive, moments of time. On the other hand, poetry can represent both space and time and action can be described in a sequence of time and expanse of space to create a cumulative totality of effect of bodies in motion. This difference is so great that it elevates poetry to a status higher than that of painting.

One more difference relates to the respective groups to which they belong: painting is an art of the eye and poetry is an art of the ear and the eye; the latter by virtue of the poet's ability of mental aspect to bring up visual pictures or images, through artistic devices. Lacking 'motion' or movement the painter can, at best, show emotions through colours and figures. But continuity of emotions or emotional changes in a progressive action cannot be depicted by the painter, as he is restrained by the rules of his art. The poet, on the other hand, adds sounds/music to motion, thereby borrowing from the fine art of music, to achieve his aim in a large measure. Moreover, nothing seems to impair the poet's art and his artistry.

A painter, conscious of his art's want of movement, can only have subjects of inanimate and vegetable kingdom, such as flowers, fruits or landscapes and animal figures, birds and human beings in a static state. Poetic imitation includes everything, which is 'performed' either by description or through music or both. The material of the poet is 'words', which serves as symbols or sounds with their rules of intonation.

Moreover, as Aristotle explains, a poet can represent actions in its different stages of progress, such as the beginning, the middle and the end with a close relationship between each stage. Painting cannot depict the time before and after the particular moment of time.

To the superiority of the art of painting over poetry, it could be stated that in the matter of the minutest details of a body in response, painting surpasses poetry, for a poet cannot, without causing monotony of description, represent minutest details of action. Poetry excels in appeals to listeners in its broader details; painting excels in its appeal, more than poetry in depicting through colours, the minute aspects of emotion.

Lessing held poetry superior to painting and other fine arts by saying that poetry is characterized by certain modes of expression and painting by certain modes of expression peculiar to each. So, poetry is not a speaking picture and painting is not mute poetry. Lessing's observations point out the truth that the laws of painting and the laws of poetry are different. Scott James says: "A practitioner in one art may doubtless borrow much that belongs to another, but he cannot borrow its medium; by the medium he uses, he is bound."

(3) Theory of Imitation

Theory of Imitation or Mimesis views the literary work as an imitation, or reflection,or representation of the world and human life, and the primary criterion applied to a work is the "truth" of its representation to the subject matter that it represents, or should represent. This mode of criticism, which first appeared in Plato and (in a qualified way) in Aristotle, remains characteristic of modern theories of literary realism.

Mimesis, the Greek word of imitation, has been a central term in aesthetic and literary theory since Plato. It is the earlier way to judge any work of art in relation to reality whether the representation is accurate or not. Though this mode starts from Plato, it runs through many great theorists of Renaissance up to some modern theorists as well. A literary work is taken to be reproducing an external reality or any aspect of it, and mimetic criticism insists on the issue that literary work does not reflect reality exactly,as it is normally believed.

Greek mimetic school is based upon the ideas expressed by Plato and Aristotle. Plato is the first major figure in the history of western philosophy. He is an idealist, moralist and a rationalist. He locates reality in what he calls ideas or forms rather than the world of appearance that we locate with our senses. Plato believes in the idea that is form which itself is formless but it is fixed. Idea is archetype and always remains the same. Reality can't be found in the world of appearance but in the ideal world. Plato, therefore, regards the painter's work as thrice removed from the "essential nature" of a thing: the artist imitates the physical object, which is a faint copy of ideas of the thing. Plato claims that art does not represent truth, it nourishes people's feelings rather than reason. In Plato's ideal 'Republic,' poets had no place. He sought to banish them from the city state.

Aristotle, on the other hand, treats imitation as a basic human faculty, which expresses itself in a wide range of arts. For him, to imitate is not to produce a copy or mirror reflection of some things but involves a complex mediation of reality. For example, in tragedy the writer imitates people's actions rather than their characters. For him, this world is real but incomplete so poet endeavors to complete it through the imitation. Thus, poets are both imitators and creators. Aristotle's poetics is a reply to Plato's Republic. He defines art is perfecting the imperfect nature. Aristotle avoids Plato's idea that the world of appearance is merely an ephemeral copy of the changeless ideas.

This school also imitates the external world but the imitation is of ancient Greek and Roman, and on purpose. This school takes imitation to be just an instrument to get to the purpose or destination; that is to teach and delight readers. Horace and Longinus are the representative figures of this school. Later on the idea that art imitates reality was developed and applied to literature and the visual arts during the Renaissance and the Enlightenment. The Neoclassicism of the 17th and the 18th century England continued the views, though in a rather modified way, of classicists like Aristotle.

Literature in the Real World

The goal of mimetic criticism is to determine how well a work of literature connects with the real world, and the theory can be broadened to include approaches that deal with the spiritual and symbolic, the images that connect people of all times and cultures. Mimetic criticism can include aspects of moral or philosophical and psychological as well. Mimetic criticism also argues that art conveys universal truths instead of just temporal and individual truths. Mimetic critics ask how well the work of literature accords with the real world. They analyse the accuracy of a literary work and its morality. They consider whether or not it shows how people really act, and whether or not it is correct. The mimetic critic assesses a literary work through the prism of his or her own time, judging the text according to his own value system.

Mimetic criticism at its best praises literary works of authors like Homer, Shakespeare and Goethe for expressing the highest ideas and aspiration of humankind. Representatives of the Mimetic Theory of Literary Criticism include Plato, Samuel Johnson, Matthew Arnold and Leo Tolstoy. Samuel Johnson argued that Shakespeare portrayed universal character traits and moral values.

Aristotle's Theory of Imitation: A Glance at the *Poetics*

Aristotle did not invent the term "imitation". Plato was the first to use the word in relation with poetry, but Aristotle breathed into it a new definite meaning. So poetic imitation is no longer considered mimicry, but is regarded as an act of imaginative creation by which the poet, drawing his material from the phenomenal world, makes something new out of it.

In Aristotle's view, principle of imitation unites poetry with other fine arts and is the common basis of all the fine arts. It thus differentiates the fine arts from the other category of arts. While Plato equated poetry with painting, Aristotle equates it with music. It is no longer a servile depiction of the appearance of things, but it becomes a representation of the passions and emotions of men which are also imitated by music. Thus Aristotle by his theory enlarged the scope of imitation. The poet imitates not the surface of things but the reality embedded within. In the very first chapter of the Poetic, Aristotle says:

Epic poetry and Tragedy, Comedy also and Dithyrambic poetry, as also the music of the flute and the lyre in most of their forms, are in their general conception modes of imitation. They differ however, from one another in three respects - their medium, the objects and the manner or mode of imitation, being in each case distinct.

The medium of the poet and the painter are different. One imitates through form and colour, and the other through language, rhythm and harmony. The musician imitates through rhythm and harmony. Thus, poetry is more akin to music. Further, the manner of a poet may be purely narrative, as in the Epic, or depiction through action, as in drama. Even dramatic poetry is differentiated into tragedy and comedy accordingly as it imitates man as better or worse.

Aristotle says that the objects of poetic imitation are "men in action". The poet represents men as worse than they are. He can represent men better than in real life based on material supplied by history and legend rather than by any living figure. The poet selects and orders his material and recreates reality. He brings order out of Chaos. The irrational or accidental is removed and attention is focused on the lasting and the significant. Thus he gives a truth of an ideal kind. His mind is not tied to reality:

It is not the function of the poet to relate what has happened but what may happen - according to the laws of probability or necessity.

History tells us what actually happened; poetry what may happen. Poetry tends to express the universal, history the particular. In this way, he exhibits the superiority of poetry over history. The poet freed from the tyranny of facts, takes a larger or general view of things, represents the universal in the particular and so shares the philosopher's quest for ultimate truth. He thus equates poetry with philosophy and shows that both are means to a higher truth. By the word 'universal' Aristotle signifies:

How a person of a certain nature or type will, on a particular occasion, speak or act, according to the law of probability or necessity.

The poet constantly rises from the particular to the general. He studies the particular and devises principles of general application. He exceeds the limits of life without violating the essential laws of human nature.

Elsewhere Aristotle says, "Art imitates Nature". By 'Nature' he does not mean the outer world of created things but "the creative force, the productive principle of the universe." Art reproduce mainly an inward process, a physical energy working outwards, deeds, incidents, situation, being included under it so far as these spring from an inward, act of will, or draw some activity of thought or feeling. He renders men, "as they ought to be".

The poet imitates the creative process of nature, but the objects are "men in action". Now the 'action' may be 'external' or 'internal'. It may be the action within the soul caused by all that befalls a man. Thus, he brings human experiences, emotions and passions within the scope of poetic imitation. According to Aristotle's theory, moral qualities, characteristics, the permanent temper of the mind, the temporary emotions and feelings, are all action and so objects of poetic imitation.

Poetry may imitate men as better or worse than they are in real life or imitate as they really are. Tragedy and epic represent men on a heroic scale, better than they are, and comedy represents men of a lower type, worse than they are. Aristotle does not discuss the third possibility. It means that poetry does not aim at photographic realism.

Aristotle by his theory of imitation answers the charge of Plato that poetry is an imitation of "shadow of shadows", thrice removed from truth, and that the poet beguiles us with lies. Plato condemned poetry that in the very nature of things poets have no idea of truth. The phenomenal world is not the reality but a copy of the reality in the mind of the Supreme. The poet imitates the objects and phenomena of the world, which are shadowy and unreal. Poetry is, therefore, "the mother of lies".

Aristotle, on the contrary, tells us that art imitates not the mere shows of things, but the 'ideal reality' embodied in very object of the world. The process of nature is a 'creative process'; everywhere in 'nature there is a ceaseless and upward progress' in everything, and the poet imitates this upward movement of nature. Art reproduces the original not as it is, but as it appears to the senses. Art moves in a world of images, and reproduces the external, according to the idea or image in his mind. Thus the poet does not copy the external world, but creates according to his 'idea' of it. Thus even an ugly object well-imitated becomes a source of pleasure. We are told in "The Poetics":

Objects which in themselves we view with pain, we delight to contemplate when reproduced with minute fidelity; such as the forms of the most ignoble animals and dead bodies.

The real and the ideal from Aristotle's point of view are not opposites; the ideal is the real, shorn of chance and accident, a purified form of reality. And it is this higher 'reality' which is the object of poetic imitation. Idealization is achieved by divesting the real of all that is accidental, transient and particular. Poetry thus imitates the ideal and the universal; it is an "idealized representation of character, emotion, action - under forms manifest in sense." That is why Aristotle defines tragedy as follows:

Tragedy, then, is an imitation of an action that is serious, complete, and of a certain magnitude; in language embellished with each kind of artistic ornament, the several kinds being found in separate parts of the play; in the form of action, not of narrative; through pity and fear effecting the proper purgation of these emotions.

Thus Aristotle successfully and finally refuted the charge of Plato and provided a defence of poetry which has ever since been used by lovers of poetry in justification of their Muse. He breathed new life and soul into the concept of poetic imitation and showed that it is, in reality, a creative process.

(4) Poetic Truth and Historical Truth

In Chapter 9 of the Poetics, Aristotle discusses the Poetic Truth and Historical Truth. Plato wanted to banish poets from his ideal Republic because poetry, according to him, was twice removed from reality and therefore false. In order to bring out the value of poetry to man's life and his understanding of life, Aristotle clarified the difference between historical truth and poetic truth. He said that history relates to what has happened, and hence a historian cannot idealize or exaggerate or underestimate the facts. History is a record of actual events, which are subject to the order of time or chronology. These events always follow the laws of cause and effect. Historical truth relates to the particular and hence it cannot be universal.

On the contrary poetic truth relates not to what happens but to what might happen. As poetry deals with incidences that might happen, the truth that poetry presents has the potential to become universal. Poetry transforms facts into permanent, timeless universal truths. Poetry transcends the world of reality to present a world that helps human mind conceive reality and human nature much better. Aristotle explains this when he says that poetic truth obeys the laws of probability and necessity. Poetry underlines the laws of life that are probable and necessary. The poet gives what is probable and possible suggesting its universality. Therefore poetic truth is more powerful than historical truth. Hence critics say that probable impossibilities are preferable to improbable possibilities. Aristotle explains the quality of poetic truth through a discussion of Sophocles' ideal tragedy *Oedipus Rex.*

The poet and the historian differ not by writing in verse or in prose. The work of Herodotus might be put into verse, and it would still be a species of history, with metre no less than without it. The true difference is that one relates what has happened, the other what may happen. Poetry, therefore, is a more philosophical and a higher thing than history: for poetry tends to express the universal, history the particular. By the universal I mean how a person of a certain type on occasion speak or act, according to the law of probability or necessity; and it is this universality at which poetry aims in the names she attaches to the personages.

History tells us what actually happened; poetry what may happen. Poetry tends to express the universal, history the particular. In this way, he exhibits the superiority of poetry over history. The poet freed from the tyranny of facts, takes a larger or general view of things, represents the universal in the particular and so shares the philosopher's quest for ultimate truth. He thus equates poetry with philosophy and shows that both are means to a higher truth which is 'universal.' Poetic truth, therefore, is higher than historical truth. Poetry is more philosophical, more conducive to understanding than Philosophy itself.

This discussion of poetic truth has continued after Aristolte. Critics have explained the nature of poetic truth. In the recent past, the subject was taken up in contemporary criticism by I.A. Richards. He discussed it at length with the poet-critic T.S. Eliot. He however tried to show how poetic truth is different from scientific truth. Whereas the latter are verifiable, the former have to be accepted on their own, without verifiability of any sort. He used the term "Pseudo statement" to refer to this ability of poetry. The term was invented by the British critic I. A. Richards in *Science and Poetry* (1926) in an attempt to distinguish the special kind of 'truth' provided by poetry and fiction: whereas scientific or ordinary 'referential' language makes statements that are either true or false, poetry's 'emotive' language gives us pseudo statements, i.e. utterances that are not subject to factual verification but which are valuable in 'organizing our attitudes'. The term proved to be controversial, partly because it was misunderstood to mean 'falsehood', and partly because it implied that poetry can have no cognitive status; but the idea itself is traditional: Sir Philip Sidney's *Apology for Poetry* (1595) argued that the poet 'nothing affirms, and therefore never lieth'.

(5) Qualifications of a Good Critic

An examination of the qualifications of a good or an ideal critic will have to be undertaken only in the light of what we expect of a good critic and what is his role in literary criticism. A good critic, on the basis of wide range and depth of his reading of literature and his catholic literary taste, functions as a dependable guide, an interpreter and a judge of literary works, finally to become a generaliser who is able to formulate his own principles of art and literature so as to mould the literary taste of his times. Let us discuss the qualifications of a good critic in the light of our expectations that he fulfils through one or more of these functions or the roles he plays.

The intrinsic qualifications that a critic should possess include a wide and many-sided reading of literature. Just as experience helps a person become mature on the path of life, a wide ranging and in-depth reading of literature makes a critic more sound and dependable in his literary responses. Such reading enables a critic to recognize the qualities of a literary genius who shows a departure in his writing from literary tradition and conventional writing. A critic has to recognize a genius, or what Eliot calls an individual talent, on first meeting him in his works. He should be quick in responding to fresh and virgin sensibility. A proper estimate of an author always takes time, but a good critic comes up with it when he comes across a literary genius for the first time.

A good critic is valuable therefore in evaluating contemporary works or books published recently. Most of the review writes perform this function. A good reviewer should possess the essential qualifications for a good critic to guide readers on the right path. Of course, we would be wrong in restricting the qualities of a good critic within the purview of contemporary literature only. Reassessment of literature and literary tradition of the past is also a fundamental task of a good critic. Eliot's reassessment of metaphysical poets and Elizabethan and Jacobean dramatists, which proves his worth as a good critic, is also valuable literary criticism. Revaluation of the past is the built-in ability expected of a critic.

In addition to wide and perceptive reading, a critic should possess a catholic taste - that ingrained aesthetic sense that distinguishes the grain from the chaff, the bad from the good, the good from the better and finally stamps the best. Without such a catholic taste, mere wide reading would be of no use. The critic, however, has to exercise his catholic taste while responding to literary works without prejudice, because subjectivity is always likely to be found in personal preferences.

A spirit of detachment has to evolve in a critic so that he would not succumb to the pressures of personal likes and dislikes. The more sincere and honest a critic is in his vocation, the greater will be his objectivity in reviewing works of art. Yet we have to accept his limitations. Dr. Johnson's inability to appreciate Milton's *Lycidas* and other shorter poems is compensated in way by his sound and balanced estimate of *Paradise Lost*. One should not underrate a critic's qualities on the basis of the few blind spots in his otherwise sensitive response. If Charles Lamb is a worthwhile critic only in connection with romantic literature, we should appreciate this quality as his strength and therefore accept his limitations with regard to the rest of the literature. A good critic always has such limitations; we should expect him to be good within his own limited range.

Although a critic is expected to be a judge, his basic function is to interpret a work of art. An ideal critic does not confine himself to judgment only. He is, first and foremost, an interpreter of literature. Endowed with a fine sensibility and an analytical mind, he is able to offer an unprejudiced interpretation of a work of art, and finally it is his interpretive skill that enables him to pass a judgment on that work of art. He, in fact, opens the entire world of imaginative experience of the work in question, enabling us to respond to it and thereby help us derive aesthetic pleasure from it. G. Wilson's Knight's analysis of Shakespeare's language or Caroline Spurgeon's brilliant study of Shakespearean imagery takes us to the heart of his plays. Many scholars considered Shakespeare's last plays as less artistic and neglected them as romances, but it was to the credit of Derek Traversi to bring out and prove the artistic merit of Shakespeare's last plays like *The Tempest*. Through their methods of analyses are different, all these critics are good in their own way. Even if the new critics have disapproved the critical methods of Prof. Livingstone Lowes used in his book on Coleridge entitled *The Road to Xanadu*, the light it throws on Coleridge's poems like *Kubla Khan* cannot be ignored. Whatever be a critic's method, it should offer a fresh insight into the work of art.

Besides being an interpreter, a critic has his own theory or philosophy of literature. We can say, a critic reaches this level when he becomes a generaliser after he reaches, through a process of deduction, a set of principles or rules that govern works of art belonging to that form or genre. The first western critic to reach this level was Aristotle.

His *Poetics* offered a set of rules or principles on the basis of his study of Greek tragic drama of his times. Most of the critics of the classical and the neo-classical era accepted Aristotle's tenets to review drama of later period. A critic always works within the theoretical framework in which he believes. Whether he is a judge, or interpreter or generaliser, a critic has to offer a fresh insights into a work of art which readers are generally likely to miss or unlikely to capture.

To conclude, we can say that wide and in-depth reading, openness of mind, ever diligent scholarly approach, an analytical mind and an attitude of judicious detachment are among the most important qualifications of a critic. An ideal critic takes his vocation as a journey, forever exploring and propagating, what Matthew Arnold calls, the best that is known and thought in the world of literature. A good critic, in short, contributes something of unique value to our appreciation of literature and our ability to recognize and enjoy the greatest and the most aesthetic quality in literature when we meet it. A good critic never expects a blind following of his views and attitudes but always teaches us to be open to what Keats refers to in the famous opening line of *Endymion:* "A thing of beauty is a joy forever."

□□

2

Critical Approaches to Literature

Although literary critics over the years have used different critical approaches to literature, it is not necessary to refer to all of them here. From the beginning, critics believed in the author as the source of the text and hence accepted biographical approach to literature. In the latter half of the 19th century, however, the sociological approach came to dominate the literature. When realism was considered inadequate by most of the writers owing to the growing interest in psychology, the psychological approach came into the vogue. In this section, these three critical approaches to literature will be discussed. Later developments in this regard, Formalistic, Linguistic, Structural and Post structural approaches to literature are not dealt with here.

1) Biographical Approach

The sole purpose of literary criticism is to get to the core of the text and discover what message the author is attempting to convey. Knowledge of an author's life and experiences can be the key to an otherwise bolted door leading to the deeper comprehension and interpretation of a literary work. Literature has more meaning and depth when we understand circumstances which prompted the writer to write. An author's experiences, along with many other factors, help to shape his writing. Furthermore, a work of literature holds more importance to readers if the writer has credibility for writing on a certain topic. This aspect of literary study is undertaken by biographical criticism in which, the critic compares facts of the author's life to the writing in order to find meaning. This meaning could include characters, places or events based on the author's own experiences. Biographical criticism seeks to illuminate the deeper meaning of themes, conflicts, characters, settings and literary allusions based on the author's own concerns and conflicts.

Biographical approach offers a form of literary criticism which analyzes a writer's biography to show the relationship between the author's life and their works of literature. Biographical criticism is often associated with historical-biographical criticism, a critical method that sees a literary work chiefly, if not exclusively, as a reflection of its author's life and times. This longstanding critical method dates back at least to the Renaissance period, and was employed extensively by Samuel Johnson in his *Lives of the Poets* (1779-81). It was possibly the first thorough-going exercise in biographical criticism.

This approach "begins with the simple but central insight that literature is written by actual people and that understanding an author's life can help readers more thoroughly comprehend the work." Biographical critics contend that readers can better understand a text by understanding the life and experiences of a writer. However, a biographical critic must be careful not to take the biographical facts of a writer's life too far in criticizing the works of that writer. As a biographical critic your task is to explicate the text by using insights gained from details about the author's life. In the light of the author's biography, the focus of the approach still remains on the text.

Biographical approach has two weaknesses that should be avoided. First, avoid equating the work's content with the author's life (or the character with the author); they are not necessarily the same. Second, avoid less-than-credible sources of information, particularly works that tend to be highly speculative or controversial unless verified by several sources.

Like any critical methodology, biographical criticism can be used with discretion and insight or employed as a superficial shortcut to understanding the literary work on its own terms through such strategies as formalism. Hence 19th century biographical criticism came under disapproval by the so-called New Critics of the 1920s, who coined the term "biographical fallacy" to describe criticism that neglected the imaginative genesis of literature.

A critic describes the form of taking interest in the author's biography as a 'recognition of 'otherness' - that there is an author who is different in personality and background from the reader appears to be a simple-minded proposition. Yet some critics ignore an important point here. The exploration of otherness is what literary biography and biographical criticism can do best, discovering an author as a unique individual, a discovery that puts a burden on us to reach out to recognize that uniqueness before we can fully comprehend an author's writings.

Biographical criticism shares in common with New Historicism an interest in the fact that all literary works are situated in specific historical and biographical contexts from which they are generated. Biographical Criticism, like New Historicism, rejects the concept that literary studies should be limited to the internal or formal characteristics of a literary work, and insists that it properly includes knowledge of the contexts in which the work was created. Biographical criticism stands in ambiguous relationship to Romanticism. It has often been argued that it is a development from Romanticism, but it also stands in opposition to the Romantic tendency to view literature as manifesting a "universal" transcendence of the particular conditions of its genesis.

In spite of the fact that dominant theoretical "schools" over the last forty years have pronounced against the use of biography in criticism and have even pronounced the author dead, biographical information and biographical accounts are regularly used in literary criticism to establish interpretative conclusions, to enhance readers' understanding of literary works and literary oeuvres, and/or to provide insight into the writing practices of authors. What is more, while biography has survived as a critical instrument, the theories that banished references to the author have faded away. This being the case, it may be time to raise again the question about the role of biographical accounts and biographical information in criticism. The answer to this question will be determined partly by the way in which the question is formulated. Those arguing against the employment of biographical information have made use of the concept of "legitimacy" rather than "relevance" or "usefulness." The notion that some kinds of criticism are "illegitimate" because they employ biographical information is a difficult one since this criticism often, though not always, seems useful or relevant. Usefulness and relevance are practice-based notions.

It is assumed in biographical approach that the author's life influences his or her work. Hence some of the questions posed by the critic in such a study are: What biographical facts has the author used in the text? What biographical facts has the author changed? Why?

What insights do we acquire about the author's life by reading the text? How do these facts and insights increase (or diminish) our understanding of the text? How does the text reflect the author's life? Is this text an extension of the author's position on issues in the author's life?

Biographical approach to literature suggests that knowledge of the author's life experiences can aid in the understanding of his or her work. While biographical information can sometimes complicate one's interpretation of a work, and some formalist critics (such as the New Critics) disparage the use of the author's biography as a tool for textual interpretation, learning about the life of the author can often enrich a reader's appreciation for that author's work. Biographical approach to literature was set aside first by T.S.Eliot in his famous essay, *Tradition and the Individual talent*. The view was later supported by I.A. Richards' experiment of *Practical Criticism* (1929). The view was seriously opposed by the New Critics when they objected to the use of authorial intention in the field of literary criticism. This was termed by Wimsatt and Beardsley as *The Intentional Fallacy.*

Some examples of biographical approach to Literature:

(A) In spite of this adverse criticism, biographical approach remained a significant mode of literary inquiry throughout the 20th century, particularly in studies of Charles Dickens and F. Scott Fiztgerald, among others. The method continues to be employed in the study of such authors as Steinbeck, Whitman and Shakespeare.

(B) However, the application of the biographical approach to literature proper - poetry, plays and fiction - (not to think of biography / autobiography form) brings out certain critical issues, for example, literature which is predominantly biographical. Let us consider some prominent examples :

1. Confessional poetry: If we read Robert Lowell or Sylvia Plath's poems, we have to be cautious in evaluating the poems. As the poems are directly personal in content, we should evaluate the art of poetry and not look at the content in the light of the poet's biographical details. Sylvia Plath's *Daddy* and *Lady Lazarus* are full of references to her marriage with the British poet Ted Hughes, the resultant unhappiness, Sylvia's mental breakdown, her three attempts of suicide and her subsequent death. These sensational details may overpower the reader

so as to neglect the quality of her poetry. Biographical references should not affect the proper evaluation of the poet's quality. Unfortunately a lot of criticism, in discussing biography predominantly, neglects literary qualities.

2. Robert Frost's poetry: A good deal of Frost criticism has taken note of the personality of the popular American poet. This biographical criticism has note paid enough attention to his form and poetic style.

3. A good deal of Romantic poetry has suffered from this defect. Wordsworth, Coleridge, Shelley, Byron, Keats were important because of their personal lives, not because of their poetry. Byronic hero mattered more than Byron the poet. (Even Keats was aware of the undue importance given to the poet, hence he put forth the concept of Negative Capability.) That was why Formalist critics did not approve of the research work in Prof. Livingston Lowes' book *Road to Xanadu.*

4. Ernest Hemingway's novels have been studied mainly in the context of his personal life, from his early Nick Adams short stories to his later classic, *The Old Man and the Sea.* The Hemingway Hero was given undue importance in his criticism for quite some time. The real Hemingway is in his writing; it is not the man but the novels should always matter.

2) Sociological Approach

The Sociological Approach focuses on the relationship between literature and society. Literature is always produced in a social context. Writers may affirm or criticize the values of the society in which they live, but they write for an audience and that audience is society. Through the ages the writer has performed the functions of priest, prophet and entertainer: all of these are important social roles. The social function of literature is the domain of the sociological critic. Even works of literature that do not deal overtly with social issues may have social issues as subtexts. The sociological critic is interested not only in the stated themes of literature, but also in the latent themes. Like the historical critic, the sociological critic attempts to understand the writer's environment as an important element in the writer's work. Like the moral critic, the sociological critic usually has certain values by which he or she judges literary work.

The Sociological approach to literature examines social groups, relationships, and values as they are manifested in literature.

Sociological approaches emphasize the nature and effect of the social forces that shape power relationships between groups or classes of people. Such readings treat literature as either a document reflecting social conditions or a product of those conditions. The former view brings into focus the social milieu; the latter emphasizes the work. Sociological approach examines literature in the cultural, economic and political context in which it is written or received, exploring the relationships between the artist and society. Sometimes it examines the artist's society to better understand the author's literary works; at other times, it may examine the representation of such societal elements within the literature itself.

Sociological approach assumes that social conditions and notions of cultures of humanity affect literature. Therefore some of the central and often-asked sociological questions are:

What sort of society does the author describe? How is it set up? What rules are there? What happens to people who break them? Who enforces the rules? What does the writer seem to like or dislike about this society? What changes do you think the writer would like to make in the society? And how can you tell? What sorts of pressures does the society put on its members? How do the members respond to this pressure?

Sociological criticism, then, reflects the way literature interacts with society. These critics show us how literature can function as a mirror to reflect social realities and as a lamp to inspire social ideals. Sociological Criticism is directed to understand or place literature in its larger social context; it codifies the literary strategies that are employed to represent social constructs through a sociological methodology. This critical approach analyzes how the social aspects function in literature and how literature works in society.

Sociological criticism is still a valid form of literary interpretation, however. Literature not only serves as a reflection of the social issues of its time, but it may attempt to reform them as well. Social criticism seeks to define the social situations represented in a work as well as the author's attitude towards them.

Historical View of Sociological Criticism

This critical approach is one of the oldest. In fact, Plato's views against poets had a social basis. Plato banished poets from his ideal republic or the city state because their poetry was twice removed from reality and so it had a bad impact on the would-be-citizens. This was the beginning of poetry as well as that of the social view of literature. In a way, most of the mimetic view of fine arts continued to look at art from the social point of view. After the classical period, the revival of classical criticism as Neoclassicism in the 17th century and its continuation in the 18th century Age of Sensibility had the same sociological bias. The Age of Dryden and Pope produced great social verse satires. That literature arises out of the writer's interactions with the social issues is underlined by this approach. Taine tried to present this view systematically when he stated that three different sources contribute produce literature. They are Race, Surrounding and Epoch. This created an awareness of culture and its progress. The two 19th century writers who presented this view in their writing were John Ruskin and Matthew Arnold. This ultimately led Ruskin to emphasize moral objectives of art and literature. Arnold's Culture and Anarchy stated that culture is a precondition for the rise proper of literature and literary criticism. He believed that literature moulds and is moulded by culture. Later on, this criticism developed under the impact of the economic base that was analysed thoroughly by Marx and Angels.

An Offshoot of Sociological Criticism

Social Criticism is also very similar to historical criticism in that it recognizes the influence of environment on literature. Social criticism became very popular during the Great Depression as many critics attempted to apply Marxist solutions to the overwhelming issues of poverty and class distinction. There are many subclassifications of sociological criticism, two of the most prominent being Marxist criticism and feminist criticism.

Marxist Criticism

One influential type of sociological criticism is Marxist criticism, which focuses on the economic and political elements of art, often emphasizing the ideological content of literature; because Marxist criticism often argues that all art is political, either challenging or endorsing (by silence) the status quo, it is frequently evaluative and judgmental. This tendency can lead to a misjudgement. For example, Soviet critics rated Jack London better than William Faulkner, Ernest Hemingway, Edith Wharton and Henry James, because he illustrated the principles of class struggle more clearly. Nonetheless, Marxist criticism can illuminate political and economic dimensions of literature other approaches overlook. Indeed, Marxist criticism sees history centered on a struggle between socioecenomic classes; therefore it sees literature as a result of class conflict or an outcome from the context of such a struggle.

Karl Marx (1818-1883) developed a theory of society, politics, and economics called dialectical materialism. Writing in the nineteenth century, Marx criticized the exploitation of the working classes, or proletariat, by the capitalist classes who owned the mines, factories, and other resources of national economies. Marx believed that history was the story of class struggles and that the goal of history was a classless society in which all people would share the wealth equally. This classless society could only come about as a result of a revolution that would overthrow the capitalist domination of the economy.

Central to Marx's understanding of society is the concept of ideology. As an economic determinist, Marx thought that the system of production was the most basic fact in social life. Workers created the value of manufactured goods, but owners of the factories reaped most of the economic rewards. In order to justify and rationalize this inequity, a system of understandings or ideology was created, for the most part unconsciously. Capitalists justified their taking the lion's share of the rewards by presenting themselves as better people, more intelligent, more refined, more ethical that the workers. Since literature is consumed, for the most part, by the middle classes, it tends to support capitalist ideology, at least in countries where that ideology is dominant.

Marxist critics interpret literature in terms of ideology. Writers who sympathize with the working classes and their struggle are regarded favorably. Writers who support the ideology of the dominant classes are condemned. Naturally, critics of the Marxist school differ in breadth and sympathy the way other critics do. As a result, some Marxist interpretations are more subtle than others. Take the Marxist approach to Shakespeare's *The Tempest* for example. The standard Marxist party line would be to interpret Prospero as the representative of European imperialism. Prospero has come to the island from Italy. He has used his magic (perhaps a symbol of technology) to enslave Caliban, a native of the island. Caliban resents being the servant of Prospero and attempts to rebel against his authority. Since Prospero is presented in a favorable light, the Marxist critic might condemn Shakespeare as being a supporter of European capitalist ideology. A more subtle Marxist critic might see that the play has far more complexity, and that Caliban has been invested with a vitality that makes it possible for audiences to sympathize with him. Certainly, the Marxist view of the play brings out ideas that might be overlooked by other kinds of critics and, thus, contributes to the understanding of the play.

Important contributions to Marxist criticism came from Georg Lukacs, a Hungarian critic. A staunch supporter of the social criticism and therefore of the 19th century realistic novel, Lukacs disapproved of the impact of psychology and psychoalalysis on literature in his essay "The Ideology of Modernism," wherein he stated that the modernist writing was asocial and therefore ahistorical and that it had lost a sense of perspective of history. A fresh interpretation of Marxist Ideology was given by an influential Neo-Marxist named Louis Althusser. He said that Ideology of the bourgeois class is not a 'false consciousness' as Marx and Angels had said; it dominates the proletariat classes transforming them into its subject. In fact, in the field of contemporary theory, Marxist view has influenced many critical schools like Feminist criticism and New Historicism.

3) Psychological Approach

The Psychological approach reflects the effect that modern psychology has had upon both literature and literary criticism. It is akin to biographical criticism as it looks at the author, from the point of view of psychology. Fundamental figures in psychological criticism include Sigmund Freud, whose psychoanalytic theories changed our notions of human behavior by exploring new or controversial areas like wish-fulfillment, sexuality, the unconscious, and repression as well as expanding our understanding of how language and symbols operate by demonstrating their ability to reflect unconscious fears or desires; and Carl Jung, whose theories about the unconscious are also a key foundation of mythological criticism. Psychological criticism has a number of approaches, but in general, it usually employs one or more of three approaches:

1. An investigation of the creative process of the artist: what is the nature of literary genius and how does it relate to normal mental functions? 2. The psychological study of a particular artist, usually noting how an author's biographical circumstances affect or influence their motivations and/or behavior. 3. The analysis of fictional characters using the language and methods of psychology.

The Psychological approach looks at how prevailing theories of human behavior find their way into literature. Therefore the central Psychological Questions are:

Are there any specific psychologists or psychological theories mentioned in the text? In what ways? What theories of human behavior does the writer seem to believe? How can you tell? What theories of human behavior does the writer seem to reject? How can you tell? How do people's minds work in the text? How do people think? How are their thoughts shown? In what ways do the structure and organization of the text indicate the writer's beliefs about the workings of the mind?

Such criticism aims at uncovering the working of the human mind—especially the expression of the unconscious. Possibilities include analyzing a text like a dream, looking for symbolism and repressed meaning, or developing a psychological analysis of a character. Three ideas found in the work of Sigmund Freud are particularly useful: the dominance of the unconscious mind over the conscious, the expression of the unconscious mind through symbols (often in dreams), and sexuality as a powerful force for motivating human behavior. Psychoanalytic criticism can be applied to either the author/text relationship or to the reader/text relationship. You might ask, "How is this text use or represent the unconscious mind: of the author, the characters, the reader?"

Using the theories of a particular psychoanalytic thinker, either Freud or Jung or Lacan, psychoanalytic critics see the text as if it were a kind of dream. This means that the text hides, represses its real content behind manifest content. Dream work involves, what Freud calls, condensation, displacement. The interpreter must make his or her way through the literal level to the symbolic import, the meaning the writer cannot say overtly because it would be too painful. Psychological criticism notices patterns of language beneath the surface and understands the verbal play as if the text were a patient recalling more than she/he realizes.

A psychoanalytic critic may use one of the methods:

1. See the text as an expression of the secret, repressed life of its author, explaining the textual features as symbolic of psychological struggles in the writer. This was popular before 1950 and is termed psychobiography. Such a critic more often used Freudian theory as a theoretical basis.

2. Look not to the author but to characters in the text, applying psychoanalytical theory to explain their hidden motives or psychological makeup. Such a critic might use theoretical templates such as Freudian or Lacanian psychoanalysis, among others.

3. Look at ways in which specific readers reveal their own obsessions, neuroses, etc. as they read a particular text. This would be an example in which Reader-Response critics use psycholanalysis in their interpretations.

Sigmund Freud's Psychoanalysis

The psychological approach has been one of the most productive forms of literary inquiry in the twentieth century. Developed in the late 1800s and early 1900s by Sigmund Freud (1856-1939) and his followers, psychological criticism has led to new ideas about the nature of the creative process, the mind of the artist, and the motivations of characters.

Freud's principal ideas are essential to an understanding of modern literature and criticism. Although the works of Freud consist of many complex volumes, there are four main ideas that have been so influential that it is hard to believe they were not always with us.

(1) The Unconscious

According to Freud, human beings are not conscious of all their feelings, urges, and desires because most of mental life is unconscious. Freud compared the mind to an iceberg: only a small portion is visible; the rest is below the waves of the sea. Thus, the mind consists of a small conscious portion and a vast unconscious portion.

(2) Repression

Observing the conservative, prudish upper middle classes of the late nineteenth century, Freud came to the conclusion that society demands restraint, order, and respectability and that individuals are forced to repress (or sublimate) the libidinous and aggressive drives. These repressed desires, however, emerge in dreams and in art. The artist and the dreamer are both creators; both have a need to express themselves by creating beautiful or terrifying images and narratives. But the lust and aggression may not be represented directly. This leads to the use of symbols and subtexts in dreams and literature.

(3) The Tripartite Psyche

(A) Freud's famous tripartite model of the mind in brief:

id - irrational, instinctual, vital, unconscious (contains our secret desires, darkest wishes, intense fears). Driven to fulfill wishes of pleasure principle

superego - internal censor but derived from societal control. Driven to fulfill demands of morality principle

ego - rational, logical, mostly conscious part of mind. Regulates id and comes to terms with super ego. Driven by reality principle, the Ego is the battleground for forces of the superego and the id.

(B) Explanation of the Model :

Freud developed his psychoanalytic theory around three principles: the ego, the id, and the superego. The ego is conscious and represents the part of the mind that interacts with the environment and with other people in social situations. As the conscious waking self, the ego is the reasonable, sane, and mature aspect of the mind capable of mastering impulses and dealing effectively with the stresses of daily life. Common parlance may show disrespect for the "big ego," but for Freud the supercilious attitude denoted by this phrase would, paradoxically, be an indication - of a weak ego. The id is unconscious and is comprised of the basic drives of hunger, thirst, pleasure, and aggression. The id is removed from reality, that is, from the outer world of society and environment. The id is the mind of the infant, demanding instant gratification, incapable of tolerating the delayed gratification that makes the ego socially acceptable. At first, Freud thought that the id had only one principle, the pleasure principle, also known as the libido or sex drive. However, he found he could not account for aggression, violence, and self-destructiveness without postulating a second principle, the aggressive drive, also known as the death wish. The superego is the final part of the tripartite psyche. Representing parentally instilled moral attitudes, the superego may seem to be like the conscience. Like the id, however, the superego is largely unconscious. Sometimes the superego is thought to represent an idealized image (ego-ideal) towards which the ego strives. During the normal course of development, an individual gains in ego strength and is able to master basic drives and mediate the demands of the id, the superego, and the environment.

(4) The Oedipus Complex

In Greek myth, Oedipus was a king of Thebes who, having been abandoned in childhood and consequently ignorant of his own identity, unknowingly killed his father and married his mother. The literature of the past has been reexamined in the light of psychoanalysis. Freud himself started this trend when he named a complex after Oedipus: this reinterpreted the play. In fact, the play was profoundly psychological in its original conception. As per the myth, Oedipus goes to Delphi and receives prophecies from the gods: what better way to express the working of the unconscious? Jocasta tells Oedipus that many men have dreamed of sleeping with their mothers: dreams do reveal unconscious desires. Finally, having sorted out his identity, Oedipus, blinds himself and leaves the stage to wander the world, a sadder and a wiser man. In describing the psychosexual development of children, Freud analyzed the powerful feelings that develop between mother and son. Freud believed that boys develop strong attractions to their mothers during the period of 3 to 6years, with a corresponding rivalry developing between the boy and his father. Usually these conflicts are resolved as the boy matures and develops love interests outside the home, but some neuroses of adult life are supposed to result from insufficiently resolved Oedipal conflicts.

The Oedipus Complex has been very controversial and some psychoanalysts have modified or rejected it. Alfred Adler (1870-1937), one of Freud's pupils, reinterpreted the Oedipus Complex when he developed his own theory of the Inferiority Complex. Adler believed that the primary motivation for human beings is not the libido, as Freud had posited, but the will to power. For Adler, then, the Oedipus Complex is essentially a power struggle between the boy and the father, in which the boy tries to overcome feelings of inferiority by successfully capturing the mother's attention. Adler also coined the term *masculine protest* to refer to the rebellion of by young women (and some young men) against the inferior status that women have in many societies. Masculine protest consists of aggressive behavior towards others in an attempt to allay feelings of inferiority.

Writers were interested in the powerful conflicts that arise in families long before Freud, but writers of the twentieth century exploring these conflicts in their works will be labeled Freudian whether they acknowledge the influence of Freud or not. D.H. Lawrence's *Sons and Lovers* explores the influence of a possessive mother on her sons; the same author's story "The Rocking- Horse Winner" depicts a boy who believes he can win his mother's love by being lucky in gambling on racehorses. Frank O'Connor's "My Oedipus Complex" is a humorous treatment of Freud's ideas. The same author's "Masculine Protest" makes use of the Adlerian notion of the inferiority complex.

Since the late 1940s Shakespeare's Hamlet has been interpreted as having an Oedipal Complex. The most prominent among them is Edmund Jones. He expresses love for his mother, and seems obsessed by the idea of Claudius and Gertrude sleeping together. His jealousy and aggression towards Claudius are overt. Of course, Claudius is not Hamlet's father but his stepfather. Hamlet idealizes and adores his real father. These facts do not deter the psychological interpreters. Perhaps the concept of masculine protest is as applicable to the play as the Oedipal conflict. Hamlet feels that Gertrude is weak; worse, he feels implicated in her weakness. Much of the play dwells on Hamlet's feelings of weakness and inferiority, and his aggressive behavior at the end may be interpreted as masculine protest.

Carl Jung

The psychological approach includes psychoanalytic theories of Carl Jung. Jung applied Freud's insights to society or community. Like the human unconscious, Jung believed that a social group has the collective unconscious. This idea also influenced the critic Northrop Frye who talked about Archetypes of Literature. One of the best examples of Jung's concept of the collective unconscious in literature is Eugene O'Neill's play *Emperor Jones*.

Neo-Freudian: Jacques Lacan

Jacques Lacan in following Freud's theory modified it under the influence of Structuralist views of language. For Lacan, the unconscious is structured like a language, this contrasts with Freud's view that the unconscious is chaotic. From Saussure, Lacan collects the idea that language is determined by difference. So too, is the unconscious. The idea of wholeness is illusory. Individuals are fragmented. Language conditions our unconscious, conscious minds. It constructs our sense of self.

Lacan's Tri Partite Model of Human Psyche :

1. The Imaginary Order : From birth to around 6 months we live in a world of wishes, images, united with the mother. Our self image is in flux because we don't yet differentiate. Between the age of 6 to 18 months, we enter a transitional stage, the mirror stage. We literally or metaphorically begin to see ourselves in the mirror, as a differentiated being. We recognize the separation of objects from ourselves, leading to a feeling of lack (loss of harmony). As we pass through the Imaginary order we long for the Mother, as a representation of total unity and wholeness.

2. The Symbolic Order : It is the next phase in our development. We are conscious of separation, of difference : males vs females; right vs wrong. As we learn language, it really masters us, shapes us as individuals. The father figure dominates in this phase. He represents the rules, the laws, the norms. The symbolic order represents a further remove from the mother. Entering the Symbolic order means a form of metaphorical castration for either sex. We are all cut off from the Imaginary, primordial state.

3. The Real Order: The final order is the Real. It includes the physical world; it includes everything the person is not. In the Real Order we are conscious of our perennial lack.

Impact of Psychological Approach in Literature : Some Examples

Upto the 19ᵗʰ century, most of the literary artists believed that realistic representation of life and reality in works of art was adequate. However, towards the end of the century, poets and writers began to feel that realism was not adequate tool to express the inner reality of human life. The impact of psychology and psychoanalysis gave rise to a form of novel that used the Stream of Consciousness technique. The welknown examples of the genre were James Joyce's *A Portrait of the Artist as a Young Man* and *Ullyses.* The same was handled effectively later on by Virginia Woolf in novels like *To the Light House, Mrs. Dalloway* and *The Waves.*

Although the novels of D.H. Lawrence have more or less used, unlike the Stream of Consciousness novel, conventional narrative form, the content of his novels comes under the term "Psychological Realism." Psychoanalytical criticism is the main source to study them. The content of Edgar Allen Poe's *The Fall of the House of Usher* and *A Purloined Letter* are primarily psychological. So also the famous tale of Henry James, *The Turn of the Screw*, is the story mental ups and downs of its principle character the Governess. Although there are different meaningful possibilities of the tale, it is interpreted better in psychoanalytic terms.

□□

3
Contribution of Selected Critics

1. Philip Sidney : *Apology for Poetry*

Introduction

This work has two titles based on the two printed editions. The first, *Defense of Poesy*, uses "poesy" for all literary forms, including lyric, drama, and prose. The second, *Apology for Poetry*, uses "apology" in the sense of the Greek word apologia, or "an argument in defense" of a client. In both senses, Sidney stands as an advocate for all creative writers at a crucial point in the development of English literature.

An Apology for Poetry is the most important contribution to Renaissance literary theory. Sidney advocates a place for poetry within the framework of an aristocratic state, while showing concern for both literary and national identity. Sidney responds in *Apology* to an emerging antipathy to poetry that saw works like Stephen Gosson's *The School of Abuse* (1579) come to prominence. The significance of the nobility of poetry is its power to move readers to virtuous action.

In an era of an antipathy to poetry, and puritanical belief in the corruption of literature, Sidney's defense was a significant contribution to the genre of literary criticism. He reconfigures Plato's argument against poets by saying poets are "the least liar." As an expression of a cultural attitude descending from Aristotle, Sidney, when stating that the poet "never affirmeth," makes the claim that all statements in literature are hypothetical or, to use I.A. Richards' term, pseudo-statements.

The following text is an abridged version. It is edited to highlight

Sidney's views on Superiority of poetry over other Sciences and other disciplines.

An Apology for Poetry (1595)
(The Text)

Let learned Greece, in any of her manifold sciences, be able to show me one book before Musaeus, Homer, and Hesiod, all three nothing else but poets. This did so notably show that the philosophers of Greece durst not a long time appear to the world but under the mask of poets; so Thales, Empedocles, and Parmenides sang their natural philosophy in verses; so did Pythagoras and Phocylides their moral counsels; so did Tyrtaeus in war matters; and Solon in matters of policy; or rather they, being poets, did exercise their delightful vein in those points of highest knowledge, which before them lay hidden to the world; for that wise Solon was directly a poet it is manifest, having written in verse the notable fable of the Atlantic Island, which was continued by Plato. And, truly, even Plato, whosoever well considereth shall find that in the body of his work, though the inside and strength were philosophy, the skin, as it were, and beauty depended most of poetry. . .

And even historiographers, although their lips sound of things done, and verity be written in their foreheads, have been glad to borrow both fashion and, perchance, weight of the poets; so Herodotus entitled the books of his history by the names of the Nine Muses; and both he, and all the rest that followed him, either stole or usurped, of poetry, their passionate describing of passions, the many particularities of battles which no man could affirm; or, if that be denied me, long orations, put in the months of great kings and captains, which it is certain they never pronounced. So that, truly, neither philosopher nor historiographer could, at the first, have entered into the gates of popular judgments, if they had not taken a great disport of poetry.

But since the authors of most of our sciences were the Romans, and before them the Greeks, let us, a little, stand upon their authorities; but even so far, as to see what names they have given unto this now scorned skill. Among the Romans a poet was called "vates," which is as much as a diviner, foreseer, or prophet, as by his conjoined words "vaticinium," and "vaticinari," is manifest; so heavenly a title did that excellent people bestow upon this heart-ravishing knowledge! . . .And may not I presume a little farther to show the reasonableness of this word "vates," and say, that the holy David's Psalms are a divine poem? If I do, I shall not do it without the testimony of great learned men, both ancient and modern. But even the name of Psalms will speak for me, which, being interpreted, is nothing but Songs; then, that is fully written in metre, as all learned Hebricians agree, although the rules be not yet fully found; lastly, and principally, his handling his prophecy, which is merely poetical. . .

But now let us see how the Greeks have named it, and how they deemed of it. The Greeks named him a Poet, which name hath, as the most excellent, gone through other languages; it cometh of this word 'poiein,' which is TO MAKE; wherein, I know not whether by luck or wisdom, we Englishmen have met with the Greeks in calling him "a maker," which name, how high and incomparable a title it is, I had rather were known by marking the scope of other sciences, than by any partial allegation.. ..

Only the poet, disdaining to be tied to any such subjection, lifted up with the vigour of his own invention, doth grow, in effect, into another nature; in making things either better than nature bringeth forth, or quite anew; forms such as never were in nature, as the heroes, demi-gods, Cyclops, chimeras, furies, and such like; so as he goeth hand in hand with Nature, not enclosed within the narrow warrant of her gifts, but freely ranging within the zodiac of his own wit. Nature never set forth the earth in so rich tapestry as divers poets have done; neither with so pleasant rivers, fruitful trees, sweet-smelling flowers, nor whatsoever else may make the too- much-loved earth more lovely; her world is brazen, the poets only deliver a golden....

Poesy, therefore, is an art of imitation; for so Aristotle termeth it in the word Mimesis; that is to say, a representing, counterfeiting, or figuring forth: to speak metaphorically, a speaking picture, with this end, to teach and delight.

Of this have been three general kinds: the CHIEF, both in antiquity and excellency, which they that did imitate the inconceivable excellencies of God; such were David in the Psalms; Solomon in the Song of Songs, in his Ecclesiastes, and Proverbs; Moses and Deborah in their hymns; and the writer of Job. . . The SECOND kind is of them that deal with matter philosophical; either moral, as Tyrtaeus,

Phocylides, Cato, or, natural, as Lucretius, Virgil's Georgics. . ... For these three be they which most properly do imitate to teach and delight; and to imitate, borrow nothing of what is, hath been, or shall be; but range only, reined with learned discretion, into the divine consideration of what may be, and should be. These be they, that, as the first and most noble sort, may justly be termed "vates;" so these are waited on in the excellentest languages and best understandings, with the fore-described name of poets. For these, indeed, do merely make to imitate, and imitate both to delight and teach, and delight to move men to take that goodness in hand, which, without delight they would fly as from a stranger; and teach to make them know that goodness whereunto they are moved; which being the noblest scope to which ever any learning was directed, yet want there not idle tongues to bark at them.

These be subdivided into sundry more special denominations; the most notable be the heroic, lyric, tragic, comic, satyric, iambic, elegiac, pastoral, and certain others; some of these being termed according to the matter they deal with; some by the sort of verse they like best to write in; for, indeed, the greatest part of poets have apparelled their poetical inventions in that numerous kind of writing which is called verse.

The philosopher, therefore, and the historian are they which would win the goal, the one by precept, the other by example; but both, not having both, do both halt. For the philosopher, setting down with thorny arguments the bare rule, is so hard of utterance, and so misty to be conceived, that one that hath no other guide but him shall wade in him until he be old, before he shall find sufficient cause to be honest. For his knowledge standeth so upon the abstract and general, that happy is that man who may understand him, and more happy that can apply what he doth understand. On the other side the historian, wanting the precept, is so tied, not to what should be, but to what is; to the particular truth of things, and not to the general reason of things; that his example draweth no necessary consequence, and therefore a less fruitful doctrine.

Now doth the peerless poet perform both; for whatsoever the philosopher saith should be done, he giveth a perfect picture of it, by some one by whom he pre-supposeth it was done, so as he coupleth the general notion with the particular example. A perfect picture, I say; for he yieldeth to the powers of the mind an image of that whereof the philosopher bestoweth but a wordish description, which doth neither strike, pierce, nor possess the sight of the soul, so much as that other doth. For as, in outward things, to a man that had never seen an elephant, or a rhinoceros, who should tell him most exquisitely all their shape, colour, bigness, and particular marks? or of a gorgeous palace, an architect, who, declaring the full beauties, might well make the hearer able to repeat, as it were, by rote, all he had heard, yet should never satisfy his inward conceit, with being witness to itself of a true living knowledge; but the same man, as soon as he might see those beasts well painted, or that house well in model should straightway grow, without need of any description, to a judicial comprehending of them; so, no doubt, the philosopher, with his learned definitions, be it of virtue or vices, matters of public policy or private government, replenisheth the memory with many infallible grounds of wisdom, which, notwithstanding, lie dark before the imaginative and judging power, if they be not illuminated or figured forth by the speaking picture of poesy...

For conclusion, I say the philosopher teacheth, but he teacheth obscurely, so as the learned only can understand him; that is to say, he teacheth them that are already taught. But the poet is the food for the tenderest tomachs; the poet is, indeed, the right popular philosopher. Whereof AEsop's tales give good proof; whose pretty allegories, stealing under the formal tales of beasts, make many, more beastly than beasts, begin to hear the sound of virtue.

But now may it be alleged, that if this managing of matters be so fit for the imagination, then must the historian needs surpass, who brings you images of true matters, such as, indeed, were done, and not such as fantastically or falsely may be suggested to have been done. Truly, Aristotle himself, in his Discourse of Poesy, plainly determineth this question, saying, that poetry is more philosophical and more ingenious than history. His reason is, because poesy dealeth with the universal consideration, and the history with the particular. . .

I conclude, therefore, that he excelleth history, not only in furnishing the mind with knowledge, but in setting it forward to that which deserves to be called and accounted good: which setting forward, and moving to well-doing, indeed, setteth the laurel crowns upon the poets as victorious; not only of the historian, but over the philosopher, howsoever, in teaching, it may be questionable. For suppose it be granted, that which I suppose, with great reason, may be denied, that the philosopher, in respect of his methodical proceeding, teach more perfectly than the poet, yet do I think, that no man is so much 'philophilosophos' as to compare the philosopher in moving with the poet. And that moving is of a higher degree than teaching, it may by this appear, that it is well nigh both the cause and effect of teaching; for who will be taught, if he be not moved with desire to be taught? And what so much good doth that teaching bring forth (I speak still of moral doctrine) as that it moveth one to do that which it doth teach. For, as Aristotle saith, it is not gnosis but praxis must be the fruit: and how 'praxis' can be, without being moved to practise, it is no hard matter to consider.

Now, therein, of all sciences (I speak still of human and according to the human conceit), is our poet the monarch. For he doth not only show the way, but giveth so sweet a prospect into the way, as will entice any man to enter into it; nay, he doth, as if your journey should lie through a fair vineyard, at the very first give you a cluster of grapes, that full of that taste you may long to pass farther. He beginneth not with obscure definitions, which must blur the margin with interpretations, and load the memory with doubtfulness, but he cometh to you with words set in delightful proportion, either accompanied with, or prepared for, the well-enchanting skill of music; and with a tale, forsooth, he cometh unto you with a tale which holdeth children from play, and old men from the chimney-corner; and, pretending no more, doth intend the winning of the mind from wickedness to virtue; even as the child is often brought to take most wholesome things, by hiding them in such other as have a pleasant taste; which, if one should begin to tell them the nature of the aloes or rhubarbarum they should receive, would sooner take their physic at their ears than at their mouth....

By these, therefore, examples and reasons, I think it may be manifest that the poet, with that same hand of delight, doth draw the mind more effectually than any other art doth. And so a conclusion not unfitly ensues; that as virtue is the most excellent resting-place for all worldly learning to make his end of, so poetry, being the most familiar to teach it, and most princely to move towards it, in the most excellent work is the most excellent workman....

Since, then, poetry is of all human learnings the most ancient, and of most fatherly antiquity, as from whence other learnings have taken their beginnings; since it is so universal that no learned nation *doth despise it, nor barbarous nation is without it; since both Roman and Greek gave such divine names unto it. the one of prophesying, the other of making, and that indeed that name of making is fit for him, considering, that where all other arts retain themselves within their subject, and receive, as it were, their being from it, the poet only, only bringeth his own stuff, and doth not learn a conceit out of a matter, but maketh matter for a conceit; since neither his description nor end containeth any evil, the thing described cannot be evil; since his effects be so good as to teach goodness, and delight the learners of it; since therein (namely, in moral doctrine, the chief of all knowledges) he doth not only far pass the historian, but, for instructing, is well nigh comparable to the philosopher; for moving, leaveth him behind him; since the Holy Scripture (wherein there is no uncleanness) hath whole parts in it poetical, and that even our Saviour Christ vouchsafed to use the flowers of it; since all his kinds are not only in their united forms, but in their severed dissections fully commendable; I think, and think I think rightly, the laurel crown appointed for triumphant captains, doth worthily, of all other learnings, honour the poet's triumph.*

Study Material

1. Highlights of *Apology:* A Summary

Sidney clearly had been contemplating the problem of the poet's role in society for a long time, perhaps since his earliest education in which he would have encountered Plato's famous banishment of poets from the ideal Republic on the grounds that they could lead the guardians and citizens to immorality. It has been argued for a long time that he may have been responding to Stephen Gosson, a Puritan pamphleteer whose School of Abuse blames playwrights and the theatre in particular, and poets in general for leading English society astray. Gosson dedicated the pamphlet to Sidney without asking permission, and some poets at the time suspected Sidney would reply in some fashion.

In the "Defense," Sidney argues that poets were the first philosophers, that they first brought learning to humanity, and that they have the power to conceive new worlds of being and to populate them with new creatures. According to Sidney, their "golden" world of possibility is superior to the "brazen" one of historians who must be content with the mere truth of happenstance. He then defines what he believes to be the essential formal characteristics of the various genres of poetry, and defends poetry against the charge that it is composed of lies. The following points highlight Sidney's "Defense."

1. Poetry needs to be defended as it has come under attack.

2. Poetry has been man's first source of inspiration. Great philosophers have been poets, including Plato and poetry in Greek and Roman times meant "Maker".

3. Whereas all philosophers, natural and moral, follow nature, only the poet grows in effect into another nature, makes things either better than nature, or makes new forms that were never there in nature.

4. The poet as a creator: The poet's talents stem from the fact that he is able to create from a pre-existing idea called the fore-conceit. Poetry is the link between the real and the ideal worlds. Poets therefore take part in the divine act of creation. Sidney says, "Nature's world is so brazen, the poets only deliver a golden."

5. The artist's skill lies in the idea or fore-conceit of the work, not in the work itself. The poet has that *idea* is so clear. He delivers those ideas as he imagines them. But it is not like building castles in the air, it is substantial.

6. Sidney's definition of poetry: "Poetry therefore is an art of imitation, for so Aristotle terms it in the word mimesis-that is to say a representing, counterfeiting, or figuring forth to speak metaphorically, a speaking picture with this end, to teach and delight."

7. Sidney points out the essential quality of the poet when he says, "It is not rhyming and versing that maketh a poet . . . But it is that feigning of notable images of virtues, vices, or what else, with that delightful teaching, which must be the right describing note to know a poet by."

8. Poetry therefore has been the most ancient of all human learning; it is our great antiquity, the source of all our learning. It is so universal that no learned nation despises it.

9. The ultimate end of poetry is to draw us to as high perfection as our degenerate souls can be made capable of. Through this effort Man can enjoy what makes him divine. Poetry has a moral purpose, therefore, consisting in leading men to truth by integrating, not dividing knowledge.

10. History teaches and so does philosophy, but the poet is superior to both, since history deals with facts and records, ultimately hearsay, and the philosopher describes abstractions that often do not relate to the world as most people understand it.

11. The peerless poet performs both the functions of the philosopher and the historian. The poet affects our feelings and does not just give examples. The philosopher teaches, but he teaches them that which is already taught. The poet is the right popular philosopher. Sidney therefore says, "Poetry is more philosophical than history, as the historian is trapped with facts. The poet uses the facts of the historian, but he makes them nobler by using the imagination in the creative process. The poet then can teach virtue-which is one of the central functions of tragedy."

12. "Now therein of all sciences is our poet the monarch." He does not begin with obscure definitions, which must blur the margin with interpretations, and load the memory with doubtfulness, but he comes to you with words set in delightful proportion accompanied with the sweet enchanting skill of music. He gives you stories that win your minds from wickedness to virtue.

13. The poet affirms nothing and therefore he never lies. Sidney says, "But the poet never affirmeth, so wise readers of poetry will never give the lie to things not affirmatively but allegorically and figuratively written."

14. The poet moves men: philosophers teach as well, but the poet can move men to desire the good for action is greater than knowledge. Thus the philosopher is concerned not only with the end (truth), but making the means of achieving this end pleasant. Poetry is even capable of making the unpleasant like war and horror pleasant in terms of the means through which it is presented. This suggests the importance of the creative process in writing poetry.

2. Relevance and Significance of Sidney's *Apology*

In "An Apology for Poetry" Philip Sidney attempts to reassert the fundamental importance of literature to society in general as well as to other creative and intellectual endeavors. Though Sidney's work does provide a synthesis of much Greek and Roman literary theory, his argument aspires to go beyond an academic debate. Literature can "teach and delight" in a manner which other methods of communication do not possess . The moral/ethical impact any literary text has upon a reader is of paramount importance to Sidney. The argument Sidney presents and develops is built around the assumption that literature has the capacity to teach most effectively and to demonstrate virtue. Let us try to understanding this claim.

Sidney places literature in an hierarchical relationship with all other forms of learning; literature inhabits the highest and most influential tier. Literature is "the first light-giver to ignorance", and from it all other sources of knowledge have been nurtured. Though an ardent admirer of Platonic philosophy, Sydney, in order to serve his intellectual exercise, rewrites or rehabilitates Plato's harsh stance on the worthlessness of literature. Unlike Plato's poet who perpetuates images far removed from the Truth, Sidney's poet can dip into the world of Forms, the Ideal, and provide us with knowledge of virtue. While the tangible world of appearances "is brazen, the poets only deliver a golden."

Against the established disciplines of history and philosophy, Sidney also uses a revision of Aristotle's Poetics to help demonstrate how literature mediates the interests of both forms of knowledge in order to teach virtue. Where philosophy deals solely with the universal, history is consumed with the particular. Literature is able to deal with the same abstract moral/ethical concepts with which philosophy grapples by providing examples rooted in concrete, although fictionalized, details. History is too concerned with the accurate recording of facts to make any conjectures on such broad concepts. Literature exists between and above history and philosophy because the knowedge of the good it conveys is the best and most useful. As Sidney states, "no learning is so good as that which teacheth and moveth to virtue, and that none can both teach and move thereto so much as poetry."

Literature also provides a reader with ample and necessary practise in making moral/ethical judgments. A literary text provides a safe outlet for such judgments to be made, discussed, and re-examined. Personal and societal codes of behavior are shaped, both strengthened and challenged, by this practise. Literature engages the reader actively with virtue as a part of this decision making process. To enlarge the conceit, literature also expands a reader's knowledge and understanding of language in terms of style, structure, form as well. This, in turn, opens new modes of expression, new metaphors, to a reader. The ability to create new and different texts is stamped into the very nature of literature. The ability to articulate and teach virtue effectively is constantly in flux from generation to generation. Literature is constantly in demand of new metaphors in order to remain resilient and relevant.

To discuss literature in its various parts, Sidney develops a series of stylistic, structural, and thematic categories: pastoral, elegiac, iambic, satiric, comic, tragic, lyric, and heroic. Each category of literature also attempts to elicit a specific ethical response from the reader. He places more emphasis on the ethical questions posed by the works of a literary text, rather than its parts.

Sidney concludes his comprehensive defense of literature by attempting to answer various challenges to its merit and continued support. The most serious of these allegations, that literature is "the nurse of abuse, infecting us with pestilent desires", Sidney is forced to acknowledge as true to a greater or lesser extent. This might seem, at first glance, to refute or undermine the argument he has labored so long to create. Sidney, however, has qualified his praise of literature from the onset. Literature can contribute to learning virtue but does not ensure virtuous action. Because he is aware of the fact that literature can and is abused by some, Sidney describes literature as a tool with the greatest potential for good, but not an inherently virtuous invention in and of itself. The destructive qualities evoked by literature are products of the fallible fragile human beings who created it, rather than an indictment of the evil nature of all literature in general. Do not, as Sidney states, "say that poetry abuseth man's wit, but that man's wit abuseth poetry."

(2) Samuel Johnson : *Preface to Shakespeare*
Introduction
Samuel Johnson, a well-known figure of late Augustan age is considered superb for his critical work, *Preface to Shakespeare* by most

critics. Johnson's preface to *The Plays of William Shakespeare* has long been considered a classic document of English literary criticism. It ranks as one of the great works in English literary criticism. In it Johnson sets forth his editorial principles and gives an appreciative analysis of the "excellences" and "defects" of the work of the great Elizabethan dramatist. Many of his points have become fundamental tenets of modern criticism.

Harold Bloom defines "Johnson's vitality as a critic" as "always sufficiently inside Shakespeare's plays to judge them as he judges human life, without ever forgetting that Shakespeare's function is to bring life to mind". In his preface, Johnson identifies several strengths and imperfections in Shakespeare's tragedies and comedies.

According to Johnson, art should be exact representation (imitation) of general nature as Plato says that art is the imitation of nature. Also, dealing with the theme of universality, Johnson seems to believe in modern thoughts that truth has to be universal, accepted by all and common for all. Nature is represented by classicists so copying them also means copying nature. Hamlet says, "Hold up a mirror to nature", which means imitation of nature according to Platonic theory. Shakespeare is also categorized by Johnson as poet of nature.

Johnson praises Shakespeare and comments, "His drama is the mirror of life". According to Johnson, his plays are so realistic that we get practical knowledge from them. Johnson says, "Shakespeare's plays are not in the rigorous and critical sense either tragedies or comedies, but compositions of a distinct kind." According to Johnson, division of Shakespeare's plays into tragedies and comedies is wrong. Eliot shares Johnson's idea of incorrect labelling of Shakespeare's dramas as tragic, comic and historic.

He presents a mingled drama – a tragi-comedy, which provides instructions in both the ways, as a tragedy as well as a comedy. He reinforces if tragedy and comedy are mingled, the effect one wants to create on the audience is impaired. Mingling of tragedy and comedy means to represent the reality of the world as it is.

The following text of Johnson's *Preface to Shakespeare* is an abridged version. It highlights only some aspects of Shakespeare's plays, particularly Johnson's defense of Shakespeare's mingling of the tragic and comic in his plays.

Preface to Shakespeare (1765)

(The text)

The Poet, of whose works I have undertaken the revision, may now begin to assume the dignity of an ancient, and claim the privilege of established fame and prescriptive veneration. He has long outlived his century, the term commonly fixed as the test of literary merit. Whatever advantages he might once derive from personal allusions, local customs, or temporary opinions, have for many years been lost; and every topic of merriment or motive of sorrow, which the modes of artificial life afforded him, now only obscure the scenes which they once illuminated. The effects of favour and competition are at an end; the tradition of his friendships and his enmities has perished; his works support no opinion with arguments, nor supply any faction with invectives; they can neither indulge vanity nor gratify malignity, but are read without any other reason than the desire of pleasure, and are therefore praised only as pleasure is obtained; yet, thus unassisted by interest or passion, they have past through variations of taste and changes of manners, and, as they devolved from one generation to another, have received new honours at every transmission.

Nothing can please many, and please long, but just representations of general nature. . . Shakespeare is above all writers, at least above all modern writers, the poet of nature; the poet that holds up to his readers a faithful mirror of manners and of life. His characters are not modified by the customs of particular places, unpractised by the rest of the world; by the peculiarities of studies or professions, which can operate but upon small numbers; or by the accidents of transient fashions or temporary opinions: they are the genuine progeny of common humanity, such as the world will always supply, and observation will always find. His persons act and speak by the influence of those general passions and principles by which all minds are agitated, and the whole system of life is continued in motion. In the writings of other poets a character is too often an individual; in those of Shakespeare it is commonly a species. . . .

Shakespeare has no heroes; his scenes are occupied only by men, who act and speak as the reader thinks that he should himself have spoken or acted on the same occasion: Even where the agency is supernatural the dialogue is level with life. Other writers disguise the most natural passions and most frequent incidents: so that he who

contemplates them in the book will not know them in the world:
Shakespeare approximates the remote, and familiarizes the wonderful;
the event which he represents will not happen, but if it were possible,
its effects would be probably such as he has assigned; and it may be
said, that he has not only shown human nature as it acts in real
exigencies, but as it would be found in trials, to which it cannot be
exposed. This therefore is the praise of Shakespeare, that his drama is
the mirror of life; that he who has mazed his imagination, in following
the phantoms which other writers raise up before him, may here be
cured of his delirious ecstasies, by reading human sentiments in human
language; by scenes from which a hermit may estimate the transactions
of the world, and a confessor predict the progress of the passions.

His adherence to general nature has exposed him to the censure
of critics, who form their judgments upon narrower principles. Dennis
and Rhymer think his Romans not sufficiently Roman; and Voltaire
censures his kings as not completely royal. Dennis is offended, that
Menenius, a senator of Rome, should play the buffoon; and Voltaire
perhaps thinks decency violated when the Danish Usurper is represented
as a drunkard. But Shakespeare always makes nature predominate over
accident; and if he preserves the essential character, is not very careful
of distinctions superinduced and adventitious. His story requires
Romans or kings, but he thinks only on men. He knew that Rome, like
every other city, had men of all dispositions; and wanting a buffoon, he
went into the senate-house for that which the senate-house would
certainly have afforded him. He was inclined to show an usurper and a
murderer not only odious but despicable, he therefore added
drunkenness to his other qualities, knowing that kings love wine like
other men, and that wine exerts its natural power upon kings. These
are the petty cavils of petty minds; a poet overlooks the casual distinction
of country and condition, as a painter, satisfied with the figure, neglects
the drapery.

The censure which he has incurred by mixing comic and tragic
scenes, as it extends to all his works, deserves more consideration. Let
the fact be first stated, and then examined.

Shakespeare's plays are not in the rigorous and critical sense
either tragedies or comedies, but compositions of a distinct kind;
exhibiting the real state of sublunary nature, which partakes of good
and evil, joy and sorrow, mingled with endless variety of proportion

and innumerable modes of combination; and expressing the course of the world, in which the loss of one is the gain of another; in which, at the same time, the reveller is hasting to his wine, and the mourner burying his friend; in which the malignity of one is sometimes defeated by the frolic of another; and many mischiefs and many benefits are done and hindered without design.

Out of this chaos of mingled purposes and casualties the ancient poets, according to the laws which custom had prescribed, selected some the crimes of men, and some their absurdities; some the momentous vicissitudes of life, and some the lighter occurrences; some the terrors of distress, and some the gayeties of prosperity. Thus rose the two modes of imitation, known by the names of tragedy and comedy, compositions intended to promote different ends by contrary means, and considered as so little allied, that I do not recollect among the Greeks or Romans a single writer who attempted both.

Shakespeare has united the powers of exciting laughter and sorrow not only in one mind, but in one composition. Almost all his plays are divided between serious and ludicrous characters, and, in the successive evolutions of the design, sometimes produce seriousness and sorrow, and sometimes levity and laughter.

That this is a practice contrary to the rules of criticism will be readily allowed; but there is always an appeal open from criticism to nature. The end of writing is to instruct; the end of poetry is to instruct by pleasing. That the mingled drama may convey all the instruction of tragedy or comedy cannot be denied, because it includes both in its alterations of exhibition, and approaches nearer than either to the appearance of life, by showing how great machinations and slender designs may promote or obviate one another, and the high and the low co-operate in the general system by unavoidable concatenation.

It is objected, that by this change of scenes the passions are interrupted in their progression, and that the principal event, being not advanced by a due gradation of preparatory incidents, wants at last the power to move, which constitutes the perfection of dramatic poetry. This reasoning is so specious, that it is received as true even by those who in daily experience feel it to be false. The interchanges of mingled scenes seldom fail to produce the intended vicissitudes of passion. Fiction cannot move so much, but that the attention may be easily transferred; and though it must be allowed that pleasing melancholy be sometimes interrupted by unwelcome levity, yet let it be considered likewise, that melancholy is often not pleasing, and that the disturbance of one man may be the relief of another; that different auditors have different habitudes; and that, upon the whole, all pleasure consists in variety.

The players, who in their edition divided our author's works into comedies, histories, and tragedies, seem not to have distinguished the three kinds, by any very exact or definite ideas.

An action which ended happily to the principal persons, however serious or distressful through its intermediate incidents, in their opinion constituted a comedy. This idea of a comedy continued long amongst us, and plays were written, which, by changing the catastrophe, were tragedies to-day and comedies to-morrow.

Tragedy was not in those times a poem of more general dignity or elevation than comedy; it required only a calamitous conclusion, with which the common criticism of that age was satisfied, whatever lighter pleasure it afforded in its progress.

History was a series of actions, with no other than chronological succession, independent of each other, and without any tendency to introduce or regulate the conclusion. It is not always very nicely distinguished from tragedy. There is not much nearer approach to unity of action in the tragedy of "Antony and Cleopatra", than in the history of "Richard the Second". But a history might be continued through many plays; as it had no plan, it had no limits.

Through all these denominations of the drama, Shakespeare's mode of composition is the same; an interchange of seriousness and merriment, by which the mind is softened at one time, and exhilarated at another. But whatever be his purpose, whether to gladden or depress, or to conduct the story, without vehemence or emotion, through tracts of easy and familiar dialogue, he never fails to attain his purpose; as he commands us, we laugh or mourn, or sit silent with quiet expectation, in tranquillity without indifference.

When Shakespeare's plan is understood, most of the criticisms of Rhymer and Voltaire vanish away. The play of "Hamlet" is opened, without impropriety, by two sentinels; Iago bellows at Brabantio's window, without injury to the scheme of the play, though in terms which a modern audience would not easily endure; the character of Polonius is seasonable and useful; and the Grave-diggers themselves may be heard with applause.

Shakespeare engaged in dramatic poetry with the world open before him; the rules of the ancients were yet known to few; the public judgment was unformed; he had no example of such fame as might force him upon imitation, nor critics of such authority as might restrain his extravagance: He therefore indulged his natural disposition, and his disposition, as Rhymer has remarked, led him to comedy. In tragedy he often writes with great appearance of toil and study, what is written at last with little felicity; but in his comic scenes, he seems to produce without labour, what no labour can improve. In tragedy he is always struggling after some occasion to be comic, but in comedy he seems to repose, or to luxuriate, as in a mode of thinking congenial to his nature. In his tragic scenes there is always something wanting, but his comedy often surpasses expectation or desire. His comedy pleases by the thoughts and the language, and his tragedy for the greater part by incident and action. His tragedy seems to be skill, his comedy to be instinct.

The force of his comic scenes has suffered little diminution from the changes made by a century and a half, in manners or in words. As his personages act upon principles arising from genuine passion, very little modified by particular forms, their pleasures and vexations are communicable to all times and to all places; they are natural, and therefore durable; the adventitious peculiarities of personal habits, are only superficial dies, bright and pleasing for a little while, yet soon fading to a dim tinct, without any remains of former lustre; but the discriminations of true passion are the colours of nature; they pervade the whole mass, and can only perish with the body that exhibits them. The accidental compositions of heterogeneous modes are dissolved by the chance which combined them; but the uniform simplicity of primitive qualities neither admits increase, nor suffers decay. The sand heaped by one flood is scattered by another, but the rock always continues in its place.

The stream of time, which is continually washing the dissoluble fabrics of other poets, passes without injury by the adamant of Shakespeare.

If there be, what I believe there is, in every nation, a stile which never becomes obsolete, a certain mode of phraseology so consonant and congenial to the analogy and principles of its respective language as to remain settled and unaltered; this stile is probably to be sought in *the common intercourse of life, among those who speak only to be understood, without ambition of elegance. The polite are always catching modish innovations, and the learned depart from established forms of speech, in hope of finding or making better; those who wish for distinction forsake the vulgar, when the vulgar is right; but there is a conversation above grossness and below refinement, where propriety resides, and where this poet seems to have gathered his comic dialogue. He is therefore more agreeable to the ears of the present age than any other author equally remote, and among his other excellencies deserves to be studied as one of the original masters of our language.*

These observations are to be considered not as unexceptionably constant, but as containing general and predominant truth

Study Material

1. Highlights of Johnson's *Preface*: A Summary

Johnson was a progressive classicist. His *Preface* is in essence a brilliant exercise in descriptive criticism. It includes a theoretical essy on the refutation of the unities of time and place, inserted midway. It discusses the following topics—Shakespeare as a poet of nature, defence of his tragi-comedy, his 'central style', his defects, attack upon the dramatic unities, the historical background and Johnson's editorial method.

1. Shakespeare as a poet of nature: Shakespeare occupies a classic position by virtue of his relative antiquity and continuannce of esteem. He is universal in outlook because he is true to nature. His play present a just and lively image of human nature. Shakespeare has no heroes, but only human beings. His drama is a mirror upto life.

2. Defence of Tragi-comedy:Although a Neoclassicist, Johnson admires mingling of the comic and the tragic in Shakespeare. As joys and sorrows, smiles and tears, victory and defeat, good and evil coexist in human life, Shakespeare's mixing of tragic and comic elements holds a mirror to nature.

3. Shakespeare's defects: There is no poetic justice and no moral purpose in his plays.

Johnson says, 'He sacrifices virtue to convenience, and is much more careful to please than to instruct, that he seems to write without any moral purpose.' His plots are loosely constructed and that there are errors of chrnology in his plays. Finally, Shakespeare is not consistent.

4. The unities in Shakespeare: Johnson only defends the unity of action which Shakespeare follows according to Aritotle's requirements. However, he does not show regard for unities if time and place. Johnson thinks that these are not really required. It is the willing suspension of disbelief that helps the spectators appreciate the plays.

2. Strength of Shakespeare's Plays

Shakespeare was an established authority by the time of Johnson. According to Johnson, "Nothing can please many, and please long, but just representations of general nature". By nature, Johnson means the observation of reality. Johnson says that Shakespeare had the ability to provide a 'just representation of general nature'. Here, Johnson presents the idea of universality. Dr. Johnson appreciates Shakespeare because he, according to Dryden's requirement of a just and lively image of human nature, fulfils it. Shakespeare as a dramatist is praiseworthy because he does what is expected from a dramatist.

Shakespeare's writings have a main theme of good and evil, these are universal problems, and everyone agrees to these problems. All humanity faces good as well as evil so the author who uses these problems will be related to people's lives. Johnson judges Shakespeare's tragedy as "a skill" and his comedy as an 'instinct'. He thinks that the natural medium for Shakespeare is comedy not tragedy. According to him, Shakespeare had to struggle for his tragedies but still they did not reach perfection.

3. Defence of Shakespeare's mingling of the tragic and the comic

Johnson was a neo-classical critic. As such, he kept Aristotle and Horace as models before him. He was also influenced by contemporary French critics like Boileau. But in his Preface, Johnson defended Shakespeare's intermingling of the tragic and the comic in one and the same play. Even Dryden had allowed it earlier.

In replying to the charges of critics against Shakespeare, Johnson says that his plays belong to a 'distinct kind'; one can call them tragic-comedies. In doing so, he had not committed any breach of rules. In fact, Shakespeare was only presenting actual state of life on the stage. Life partakes of good and evil, joy and sorrow at the same time. Ancient writers had separated them; the plays with terror and distress were called tragedies, while others full of gaiety and prosperity were named comedies.

But Shakespeare, Johnson says, 'united the powers of exciting laughter and sorrow not only in one mind, but in one composition." By this admixture of genres, he approached actual life. In showing a character as happy at one time and full of grief at another, Shakespeare was only depicting human nature. In this, he was fulfilling the end of poetry, which is "to instruct by pleasing." Johnson's statement, 'there is always an appeal open from criticism to nature," lifts Shakespeare above the lesser neo-classical critics who insist on rules. Shakespeare's aim was to satisfy audiences of varied tastes. So Johnson defends him saying, "All pleasure consists in variety" and therefore he calls tragic-comedy a third genre.

Johnson points out that changing the dramatic action to turn a play into a tragedy or comedy forcibly was artificial. Shakespeare understood the audience's mind and their expectations. By interchanging seriousness with merriment, he softened their minds at one time and exhilarated them at another. In a way, he holds the audience in his hands, he commands them to laugh or mourn, to sit silent with expectation. The entry of Polonius in *Hamlet* achieves this effect. The audiences listen to the grave-diggers with appreciation. The porter scene relives the tension of the King's murder in *Macbeth*. Only a great artist of Shakespeare's worth was able to achieve this, Johnson endorses while defending him.

(3) Wordsworth : *Preface to Lyrical Ballads*
Introduction

Literary historians consider the *Lyrical Ballads* (1798) a seminal work in the ascent of Romanticism and a harbinger of trends in the English poetry that followed it. The poetic principles discussed by Wordsworth in the "Preface" to the 1800 edition of *Lyrical Ballads* constitute a key primary document of the Romantic era because they announce a revolution in critical notions about poetic language, poetic subject matter, and the role of the poet.

'Lyrical Ballads' is a collection of poems penned by William Wordsworth and Samuel Taylor Coleridge, published in 1798. These two poets belonged to the Romantic age and wanted to give the readers a new kind of poetry. While Wordsworth chose an ordinary subject matter for his poetry and presented it in an extraordinary manner, Coleridge opted for extraordinary subject matter which he presented in an ordinary manner.

Wordsworth's poetry was different from that of his predecessors and cotemporaries. Hence, on the advice of his friends, he added preface to the second volume of 'Lyrical Ballads', to make his poems easily understandable to the readers. William Wordsworth, a renowned Nature Poet has also proved his mettle as a critic. His contribution to literary criticism is very less but prominent.

Wordsworth and Coleridge state in the *Preface* that the poems in the collection were intended as a deliberate experiment in style and subject matter. Wordsworth elaborated on this idea in the "Preface" to the 1800 and 1802 editions which outline his main ideas of a new theory of poetry. Rejecting the classical notion that poetry should be about elevated subjects and should be composed in a formal style, Wordsworth instead championed more democratic themes- the lives of ordinary men and women, farmers, paupers, and the rural poor. In the "Preface" Wordsworth also emphasizes his commitment to writing in the ordinary language of people, not a highly crafted poetical one. True to traditional ballad form, the poems depict realistic characters in realistic situations, and so contain a strong narrative element. Wordsworth and Coleridge were also interested in presenting the psychology of the various characters in the *Lyrical Ballads*. Wordsworth also discussed the role of poetry itself, which he viewed as an aid in keeping the individual "sensitive" in spite of the effects of growing alienation in the new industrial age. The poet, as Wordsworth points out, is not a distant observer or moralist, but rather "a man speaking to men," and the production of poetry is the result of "the spontaneous overflow of powerful feelings," recollected in tranquility, not the sum total of rhetorical art.

Textual History: The first edition of *Lyrical Ballads* was published anonymously in 1798. It contained four poems by Coleridge, including *The Rime of the Ancient Mariner,* which opened the collection, with the remainder of the poems written by Wordsworth. This edition sold out in two years, and Wordsworth published a new edition, under his own name, in 1800. This second edition included the now-famous "Preface," as well as another volume of poems. Wordsworth published a third edition in 1802 with an enlarged "Preface," and a final edition 1805. The following edition of the Preface is an abridged version. It highlights Wordsworth's Definition of poetry and his views on Language of Poetry & objects of poetry.

Preface to Lyrical Ballads (1802)
(The Text)

The principal object which I proposed in these Poems was to choose incidents and situations from common life, and to relate or describe them, throughout, as far as was possible, in a selection of language really used by men; and, at the same time, to throw over them a certain colouring of imagination, whereby ordinary things should be presented to the mind in an unusual way; and, further, and above all, to make these incidents and situations interesting by tracing in them, truly though not ostentatiously, the primary laws of our nature: chiefly, as far as regards the manner in which we associate ideas in a state of excitement. Low and rustic life was generally chosen, because in that condition, the essential passions of the heart find a better soil in which they can attain their maturity, are less under restraint, and speak a plainer and more emphatic language; because in that condition of life our elementary feelings co-exist in a state of greater simplicity, and, consequently, may be more accurately contemplated, and more forcibly communicated; because the manners of rural life germinate from those elementary feelings; and, from the necessary character of rural occupations, are more easily comprehended, and are more durable; and lastly, because in that condition the passions of men are incorporated with the beautiful and permanent forms of nature. The language, too, of these men is adopted because such men hourly communicate with the best objects from which the best part of language is originally derived; and because, from their rank in society and the sameness and narrow circle of their intercourse, being less under the influence of social vanity they convey their feelings and notions in simple and unelaborated expressions. Accordingly, such a language, arising out of repeated experience and regular feelings, is a more permanent, and a far more philosophical language, than that which is frequently substituted for it by Poets, who think that they are conferring honour upon themselves and their art, in proportion as they separate themselves from the sympathies of men, and indulge in arbitrary and capricious habits of expression, in order to furnish food for fickle tastes, and fickle appetites, of their own creation.

I cannot, however, be insensible of the present outcry against the triviality and meanness both of thought and language, which some of my contemporaries have occasionally introduced into their metrical compositions; and I acknowledge, that this defect, where it exists, is more dishonorable to the Writer's own character than false refinement or arbitrary innovation, though I should contend at the same time that it is far less pernicious in the sum of its consequences. From such verses the Poems in these volumes will be found distinguished at least by one mark of difference, that each of them has a worthy purpose. Not that I mean to say, that I always began to write with a distinct purpose formally conceived; but I believe that my habits of meditation have so formed my feelings, as that my descriptions of such objects as strongly excite those feelings, will be found to carry along with them a purpose. If in this opinion I am mistaken, I can have little right to the name of a Poet. For all good poetry is the spontaneous overflow of powerful feelings: but though this be true, Poems to which any value can be attached, were never produced on any variety of subjects but by a man, who being possessed of more than usual organic sensibility, had also thought long and deeply. For our continued influxes of feeling are modified and directed by our thoughts, which are indeed the representatives of all our past feelings; and, as by contemplating the relation of these general representatives to each other we discover what is really important to men, so, by the repetition and continuance of this act, our feelings will be connected with important subjects, till at length, if we be originally possessed of much sensibility such habits of mind will be produced, that, by obeying blindly and mechanically the impulses of those habits, we shall describe objects, and utter sentiments, of such a nature and in such connection with each other, that the understanding of the being to whom we address ourselves, if he be in a healthful state of association, must necessarily be in some degree enlightened, and his affections ameliorated.

The subject is indeed important! For the human mind is capable of being excited without the application of gross and violent stimulants; and he must have a very faint perception of its beauty and dignity who does not know this, and who does not further know, that one being is elevated above another, in proportion as he possesses this capability.

It has therefore appeared to me, that to endeavour to produce or enlarge this capability is one of the best services in which, at any period, a Writer can be engaged; but this service, excellent at all times, is especially so at the present day. For a multitude of causes, unknown to former times, are now acting with a combined force to blunt the discriminating powers of the mind, and unfitting it for all voluntary exertion to reduce it to a state of almost savage torpor. . . The invaluable works of our elder writers, I had almost said the works of Shakespeare and Milton are driven into neglect by frantic novels, sickly and stupid German Tragedies, and deluges of idle and extravagant stories in verse. When I think upon this degrading thirst after outrageous stimulation, I am almost ashamed to have spoken of the feeble effort with which I have endeavoured to counteract it; and, reflecting upon the magnitude of the general evil, I should be oppressed with no dishonorable melancholy, had I not a deep impression of certain inherent and indestructible qualities of the human mind, and likewise of certain powers in the great and permanent objects that act upon it which are equally inherent and indestructible; and did I not further add to this impression a belief, that the time is approaching when the evil will be systematically opposed, by men of greater powers, and with far more distinguished success.

Having dwelt thus long on the subjects and aim of these Poems, I shall request the Reader's permission to apprize him of a few circumstances relating to their style, in order, among other reasons, that I may not be censured for not having performed what I never attempted. The Reader will find that personifications of abstract ideas rarely occur in these volumes; and, I hope, are utterly rejected as an ordinary device to elevate the style, and raise it above prose. I have proposed to myself to imitate, and, as far as is possible, to adopt the very language of men; and assuredly such personifications do not make any natural or regular part of that language. They are, indeed, a figure of speech occasionally prompted by passion, and I have made use of them as such; but I have endeavoured utterly to reject them as a mechanical device of style, or as a family language which Writers in metre seem to lay claim to by prescription. I have wished to keep my Reader in the company of flesh and blood, persuaded that by so doing I shall interest him. I am, however, well aware that others who pursue a different track may interest him likewise; I do not interfere with their claim, I only wish to prefer a different claim of my own. There will also be found in these volumes little of what is usually called poetic diction; I have taken as much pains to avoid it as others ordinarily take to produce it; this I have done for the reason already alleged, to bring my language near to the language of men, and further, because the pleasure which I have proposed to myself to impart is of a kind very different from that which is supposed by many persons to be the proper object of poetry. ...And it would be a most easy task to prove to him, that not only the language of a large portion of every good poem, even of the most elevated character, must necessarily, except with reference to the metre, in no respect differ from that of good prose, but likewise that some of the most interesting parts of the best poems will be found to be strictly the language of prose, when prose is well written.

I have shown that the language of Prose may yet be well adapted to Poetry; and I have previously asserted that a large portion of the language of every good poem can in no respect differ from that of good Prose. I will go further. I do not doubt that it may be safely affirmed, that there neither is, nor can be, any essential difference between the language of prose and metrical composition. We are fond of tracing the resemblance between Poetry and Painting, and, accordingly, we call them Sisters: but where shall we find bonds of connection sufficiently strict to typify the affinity betwixt metrical and prose composition? They both speak by and to the same organs; the bodies in which both of them are clothed may be said to be of the same substance, their affections are kindred and almost identical, not necessarily differing even in degree; Poetry sheds no tears "such as Angels weep," but natural and human tears; she can boast of no celestial Ichor that distinguishes her vital juices from those of prose; the same human blood circulates through the veins of them both. ...

If it be affirmed that rhyme and metrical arrangement of themselves constitute a distinction which overturns what I have been saying on the strict affinity of metrical language with that of prose, and paves the way for other artificial distinctions which the mind voluntarily admits, I answer that the language of such Poetry as I am recommending is, as far as is possible, a selection of the language really spoken by men; that this selection, wherever it is made with true taste and feeling, will of itself form a distinction far greater than would at first be imagined, and will entirely separate the composition from the vulgarity and meanness of ordinary life; and, if metre be superadded thereto, I believe that a dissimilitude will be produced altogether sufficient for the gratification of a rational mind. ...

Taking up the subject, then, upon general grounds, I ask what is meant by the word Poet? What is a Poet? To whom does he address himself? And what language is to be expected from him? He is a man speaking to men: a man, it is true, endued with more lively sensibility, more enthusiasm and tenderness, who has a greater knowledge of human nature, and a more comprehensive soul, than are supposed to be common among mankind; a man pleased with his own passions and volitions, and who rejoices more than other men in the spirit of life that is in him; delighting to contemplate similar volitions and passions as manifested in the goings-on of the Universe, and habitually impelled to create them where he does not find them. To these qualities he has added a disposition to be affected more than other men by absent things as if they were present; an ability of conjuring up in himself passions, which are indeed far from being the same as those produced by real events, yet do more nearly resemble the passions produced by real events, than any thing which, from the motions of their own minds merely, other men are accustomed to feel in themselves; whence, and from practice, he has acquired a greater readiness and power in expressing what he thinks and feels, and especially those thoughts and feelings which, by his own choice, or from the structure of his own mind, arise in him without immediate external excitement. ...

Aristotle, I have been told, hath said, that Poetry is the most philosophic of all writing: it is so: its object is truth, not individual and local, but general, and operative; not standing upon external testimony, but carried alive into the heart by passion; truth which is its own testimony, which gives strength and divinity to the tribunal to which it appeals, and receives them from the same tribunal. Poetry is the image of man and nature. The obstacles which stand in the way of the fidelity of the Biographer and Historian, and of their consequent utility, are incalculably greater than those which are to be encountered by the Poet, who has an adequate notion of the dignity of his art. The Poet writes under one restriction only, namely, that of the necessity of giving immediate pleasure to a human Being possessed of that information which may be expected from him, not as a lawyer, a physician, a mariner, an astronomer or a natural philosopher, but as a Man. Except this one restriction, there is no object standing between the Poet and the image of things; between this, and the Biographer and Historian there are a thousand.

....What then does the Poet? He considers man and the objects that surround him as acting and re-acting upon each other, so as to produce an infinite complexity of pain and pleasure; he considers man in his own nature and in his ordinary life as contemplating this with a certain quantity of immediate knowledge, with certain convictions, intuitions, and deductions which by habit become of the nature of intuitions; he considers him as looking upon this complex scene of ideas and sensations, and finding every where objects that immediately excite in him sympathies which, from the necessities of his nature, are accompanied by an overbalance of enjoyment. ...

He considers man and nature as essentially adapted to each other, and the mind of man as naturally the mirror of the fairest and most interesting qualities of nature. And thus the Poet, prompted by this feeling of pleasure which accompanies him through the whole course of his studies, converses with general nature with affections akin to those, which, through labour and length of time, the Man of Science has raised up in himself, by conversing with those particular parts of nature which are the objects of his studies. The knowledge both of the Poet and the Man of Science is pleasure; but the knowledge of the one cleaves to us as a necessary part of our existence, our natural and unalienable inheritance; the other is a personal and individual acquisition, slow to come to us, and by no habitual and direct sympathy connecting us with our fellow- beings. The Man of Science seeks truth as a remote and unknown benefactor; he cherishes and loves it in his solitude: the Poet, singing a song in which all human beings join with him, rejoices in the presence of truth as our visible friend and hourly companion. Poetry is the breath and finer spirit of all knowledge; it is the impassioned expression which is in the countenance of all Science. Emphatically may it be said of the Poet, as Shakespeare hath said of man, "that he looks before and after." He is the rock of defence of human nature; an upholder and preserver, carrying every where with him relationship and love. In spite of difference of soil and climate, of language and manners, of laws and customs, in spite of things silently gone out of mind and things violently destroyed, the Poet binds together by passion and knowledge the vast empire of human society, as it is spread over the whole earth, and over all time. The objects of the Poet's thoughts are every where; though the eyes and senses of man are, it is true, his favorite guides, yet he will follow wheresoever he can find an atmosphere of sensation in which to move his wings. Poetry is the first and last of all knowledge- it is as immortal as the heart of man. ...

It is not, then, in the dramatic parts of composition that we look for this distinction of language; but still it may be proper and necessary where the Poet speaks to us in his own person and character. To this I answer: by referring my Reader to the description which I have before given of a Poet. Among the qualities which I have enumerated as principally conducting to form a Poet, is implied nothing differing in kind from other men, but only in degree. The sum of what I have there said is, that the Poet is chiefly distinguished from other men by a greater promptness to think and feel without immediate external excitement, and a greater power in expressing such thoughts and feelings as are produced in him in that manner. But these passions and thoughts and feelings are the general passions and thoughts and feelings of men. ...

It will now be proper to answer an obvious question, namely, why, professing these opinions, have I written in verse? ...To this, by such as are unconvinced by what I have already said, it may be answered, that a very small part of the pleasure given by Poetry depends upon the metre. ....The end of Poetry is to produce excitement in co-existence with an overbalance of pleasure. Now, by the supposition, excitement is an unusual and irregular state of the mind; ideas and feelings do not in that state succeed each other in accustomed order. ...

If I had undertaken a systematic defence of the theory upon which these poems are written, it would have been my duty to develop the various causes upon which the pleasure received from metrical language depends. Among the chief of these causes is to be reckoned a principle which must be well known to those who have made any of the Arts the object of accurate reflection; I mean the pleasure which the mind derives from the perception of similitude in dissimilitude. This principle is the great spring of the activity of our minds, and their chief feeder. From this principle the direction of the sexual appetite, and all the passions connected with it take their origin: It is the life of our ordinary conversation; and upon the accuracy with which similitude in dissimilitude, and dissimilitude in similitude are perceived, depend our taste and our moral feelings. ...

I have said that Poetry is the spontaneous overflow of powerful feelings: it takes its origin from emotion recollected in tranquillity: the emotion is contemplated till by a species of reaction the tranquillity gradually disappears, and an emotion, kindred to that which was before the subject of contemplation, is gradually produced, and does itself actually exist in the mind. In this mood successful composition generally begins, and in a mood similar to this it is carried on; but the emotion, of whatever kind and in whatever degree, from various causes is qualified by various pleasures, so that in describing any passions whatsoever, which are voluntarily described, the mind will upon the whole be in a state of enjoyment. Now, if Nature be thus cautious in preserving in a state of enjoyment a being thus employed, the Poet ought to profit by the lesson thus held forth to him, and ought especially to take care, that whatever passions he communicates to his Reader, those passions, if his Reader's mind be sound and vigorous, should always be accompanied with an overbalance of pleasure. Now the music of harmonious metrical language, the sense of difficulty overcome, and the blind association of pleasure which has been previously received from works of rhyme or metre of the same or similar construction, an indistinct perception perpetually renewed of language closely resembling that of real life, and yet, in the circumstance of metre, differing from it so widely, all these imperceptibly make up a complex feeling of delight, which is of the most important use in tempering the painful feeling, which will always be found intermingled with powerful descriptions of the deeper passions.

Study Material

1. Highlights of Wordsworth's *Preface*: A Summary

(A) Wordsworth begins his "preface to Lyrical Ballads" by focusing on issues of style. He claims, "Humble and rustic life was generally chosen, because, in that condition, the essential passions of the heart find a better soil in which they can attain their maturity, are less under restraint, and speak a plainer and more emphatic language." He believes that feelings "coexist in a state of greater simplicity" and, as a result, are "more accurately contemplated, and more forcibly communicated." From this perspective, Wordsworth is aiming the success of poetry as an art form at the human experience. His premise depends on the notion that poetry is meant to be a communication tool first and foremost. As a result, it is the responsibility of the poet to express himself in an appropriate manner. Wordsworth is correct in assuming that unless readers can gain pleasure from reading something they do not understand; the poet should descend from his "supposed height" and "express himself as other men express themselves." This statement lies at the very heart of Wordsworth's notion.

One main point of the preface is to relate Wordsworth's intention to depict the common man, using the common language of man in his poetry. Another goal outlined in the preface is to show how feeling "gives importance to the action and the situation." A third goal of Wordsworth's poetry is to illustrate the way in which poetry is a "spontaneous overflow of powerful feelings." Wordsworth clearly achieves these goals for the most part, however seems to not fully display the way in which poetry is this "overflow of feelings."

(B) The *Preface* is divided into three main divisions:

1. Subject matter: Wordsworth chose incidents and situations from common life as subject matter. He says that he prefers rustic life because it exhibits simplicity and true human nature. A poet using his talent of imagination can turn incidents or events drawn from ordinary life into beautiful extraordinary poetry. The style of writing and the language used should be simple.

2. Function of a poet: The main purpose of a poem is not only to give pleasure to the readers but also to enlighten them with new ideas and purify their feelings. Hence it is the duty of the poet to produce good poetry. A poet endowed with an intense power of imagination and sensibility is capable of expressing his emotions and ideas precisely in` his poems. Aristotle in his 'Poetics' has said that poetic truth is higher than the truth of History or Philosophy as it supplies both particular and general truths. Poetic truth is universal which is common to all and understandable to all. Hence it is the responsibility of the poet to convey messages of love and unity, thus emphasizing oneness of all.

3. Language of poetry: Wordsworth out rightly rejects artificial and ornamental language which is known as Poetic Diction. He says

that flowery language drowns the feelings expressed in the poetry. Common man could not understand the intellectual poetry of the Neo classical age which was full of logic, reason and wit. Wordsworth advises poets to use simple rustic language but he adds that even rustic language needs to be purified of the slang.

4. Wordsworth has defined Poetry as 'the spontaneous overflow of powerful feelings, it takes its origin in emotion recollected in tranquility' and he has declared that a 'poet is a man talking to men'.

5. Wordsworth recommends using metre in poetry as it adds beauty to the poems. He says that unlike poetic diction which does not have standard rules, metre has got a regular and uniform pattern and is easily understandable.

6. Wordsworth argues that poetry should be written in the natural language of common speech, rather than in the lofty and elaborate dictions that were then considered "poetic." He argues that poetry should offer access to the emotions contained in memory. And he argues that the first principle of poetry should be pleasure, that the chief duty of poetry is to provide pleasure through a rhythmic and beautiful expression of feeling—for all human sympathy, he claims, is based on a subtle pleasure principle that is "the naked and native dignity of man."

2. Wordsworth and Coleridge: Emotion, Imagination and Complexity

The 19th century was heralded by a major shift in the conception and emphasis of literary art and, specifically, poetry. During the 18th century the catchphrase of literature and art was reason. Logic and rationality took precedence in any form of written expression. Ideas of validity and aesthetic beauty were centered on concepts such as the collective "we" and the eradication of passion in human behavior. In 1798 all of those ideas about literature were challenged by the publication of *Lyrical Ballads*, which featured the poetry of William Wordsworth and Samuel Taylor Coleridge. Wordsworth and Coleridge both had strong, and sometimes conflicting, opinions about what constituted well-written poetry. Their ideas were centered on the origins of poetry in the poet and the role of poetry in the world, and these theoretical concepts led to the creation of poetry that is sufficiently complex to support a wide variety of critical readings in a modern context.

Wordsworth wrote a preface to *Lyrical Ballads* in which he puts forth his ideas about poetry. His conception of poetry hinges on three major premises. Wordsworth asserts that poetry is the language of the common man:

Poetry should be understandable to anybody living in the world. Wordsworth eschews the use of lofty, poetic diction, which in his mind is not related to the language of real life. He sees poetry as acting like Nature, which touches all living things and inspires and delights them. Wordsworth calls for poetry to be written in the language of the "common man," and the subjects of the poems should also be accessible to all individuals regardless of class or position. Wordsworth also makes the points that "poetry is the spontaneous overflow of powerful feelings: it takes its origin from emotion recollected in tranquility." These two points form the basis for Wordsworth's explanation of the process of writing poetry. First, some experience triggers a transcendent moment, an instance of the sublime. The senses are overwhelmed by this experience; the "spontaneous overflow of powerful feelings" leaves an individual incapable of articulating the true nature and beauty of the event. It is only when this emotion is "recollected in tranquility" that the poet can assemble words to do the instance justice. It is necessary for the poet to have a certain personal distance from the event or experience being described that he can compose a poem that conveys to the reader the same experience of sublimity. With this distance the poet can reconstruct the "spontaneous overflow of powerful feelings" the experience caused within himself.

(4) Matthew Arnold : *The Study of Poetry*
Introduction

Matthew Arnold was one of the foremost poets and critics of the 19th century. While often regarded as the father of modern literary criticism, he also wrote extensively on social and cultural issues, religion, and education. He began his career as a school inspector, traveling throughout much of England on the newly built railway system. When he was elected professor of poetry at Oxford in 1857, he was the first in the post to deliver his lectures in English rather than Latin. While many have continued to disparage Arnold for his moralistic tone and literary judgments, his work has also laid the foundation for important 20th century critics like T.S. Eliot, Cleanth Brooks, and Harold Bloom.

Perhaps Arnold's most famous piece of literary criticism is his essay "The Study of Poetry." In this work, Arnold is fundamentally concerned with poetry's "high destiny;" he believes that "mankind will discover that we have to turn to poetry to interpret life for us, to console us, to sustain us" as science and philosophy will eventually prove flimsy and unstable. Arnold's essay thus concerns itself with articulating a "high standard" and "strict judgment" in order to avoid the fallacy of valuing certain poems (and poets) too highly, and lays out a method for discerning only the best and therefore "classic" poets (as distinct from the description of writers of the ancient world). Arnold's classic poets include Milton, Shakespeare, Dante, and Homer, and the passages he presents from each are intended to show how their poetry is timeless and moving. For Arnold, feeling and sincerity are paramount, as is the seriousness of subject: "The superior character of truth and seriousness, in the matter and substance of the best poetry, is inseparable from the superiority of diction and movement marking its style and manner." An example of an indispensable poet who falls short of Arnold's "classic" designation is Geoffrey Chaucer, who, Arnold states, ultimately lacks the "high seriousness" of classic poets.

At the root of Arnold's argument is his desire to illuminate and preserve the poets he believes to be the touchstones of literature, and to ask questions about the moral value of poetry that does not champion truth, beauty, valor, and clarity. Arnold's belief that poetry should both uplift and console drives the essay's logic and its conclusions.

The following summary is an abridged version of the essay in general. It highlights three kinds of estimates of poetry; the Touchstone method of evaluating poetry.

The Study of Poetry (1880)
(The text)

"The FUTURE of poetry is immense, because in poetry, where it is worthy of its high destinies, our race, as time goes on, will find an ever surer and surer stay. There is not a creed which is not shaken, not an accredited dogma which is not shown to be questionable, not a received tradition which does not threaten to dissolve. Our religion has materialized itself in the fact, in the supposed fact; it has attached

its emotion to the fact, and how the fact is failing it. But for poetry the idea is everything; the rest is a world of illusion, of divine illusion. Poetry attaches its emotion to the idea; the idea is the fact. The strongest part of our religion today is its unconscious poetry."

Let me be permitted to quote these words of my own, as uttering the thought which should, in my opinion, go with us and govern us in all our study of poetry. In the present work it is the course of one great contributory stream to the world-river of poetry that we are invited to follow. We are here invited to trace the stream of English poetry. But whether we set ourselves, as here, to follow only one of the several streams that make the mighty river of poetry, or whether we seek to know them all, our governing thought should be the same. We should conceive of poetry worthily, and more highly than it has been the custom to conceive of it. We should conceive of it as capable of higher uses, and called to higher destinies than those which in general men have assigned to it hitherto. More and more mankind will discover that we have to turn to poetry to interpret life for us, to console us, to sustain us. Without poetry, our science will appear incomplete; and most of what now passes with us for religion and philosophy will be replaced by poetry. Science, I say, will appear incomplete without it. For finely and truly does Wordsworth call poetry "the impassioned expression which is in a countenance of all science" and what is a countenance without its expression? Again, Wordsworth finely and truly calls poetry "the breath and finer spirit of all knowledge": our religion, parading evidences such as those on which the popular mind relies now; our philosophy, pluming itself on its reasonings about causation and finite and infinite being; what are they but the shadows and dreams and false shows of knowledge? The day will come when we shall wonder at ourselves for having trusted to them, for having taken them seriously; and the more we perceive their hollowness, the more we shall prize "the breath and finer spirit of knowledge" offered to us by poetry.

But if we conceive thus highly of the destinies of poetry, we must also set our standard for poetry high, since poetry, to be capable of fulfilling such high destinies, must be poetry of a high order of excellence. We must accustom ourselves to a high standard and to a strict judgment. . . For in poetry the distinction between excellent and inferior, sound and unsound or only half-sound, true and untrue or only half-true, is of paramount importance. It is of paramount importance because of the high destinies of poetry. In poetry, as a criticism of life under the conditions fixed for such a criticism by the laws of poetic truth and poetic beauty, the spirit of our race will find, we have said, as time goes on and as other helps fail, its consolation and stay. But the consolation and stay will be of power in proportion to the power of the criticism of life. And the criticism of life will be of power in proportion as the poetry conveying it is excellent rather than inferior, sound rather than unsound or half-sound, true rather than untrue or half-true.

The best poetry is what we want; the best poetry will be found to have a power of forming, sustaining, and delighting us, as nothing else can. A clearer, deeper sense of the best is the most precious benefit which we can gather from a poetical collection such as the present. And yet in the very nature and conduct of such a collection there is inevitably something which tends to obscure in us the consciousness of what our benefit should be, and to distract us from the pursuit of it. We should therefore steadily set it before our minds at the outset, and should compel ourselves to revert constantly to the thought of it as we proceed.

Yes; constantly in reading poetry, a sense for the best, the really excellent, and of the strength and joy to be drawn from it, should be present in our minds and should govern our estimate of what we read. But this real estimate, the only true one, is liable to be superseded, if we are not watchful, by two other kinds of estimate, the historic estimate and the personal estimate, both of which are fallacious. A poet or a poem may count to us historically, they may count to us on grounds personal to ourselves, and they may count to us really. They may count to us historically. The course of development of a nation's language, thought, and poetry, is profoundly interesting; and by regarding a poet's work as a stage in this course of development we may easily bring ourselves to make it of more importance as poetry than in itself it really is, we may come to use a language of quite exaggerated praise in criticising it; in short, to over-rate it. So arises in our poetic judgments the fallacy caused by the estimate which we may call historic. Then, again, a poet or a poem may count to us on grounds personal to ourselves. Our personal affinities, likings, and circumstances, have great power to sway our estimate of this or that poet's work, and to make us attach more importance to it as poetry than in itself it really possesses, because to us it is, or has been, of high importance. Here also we over-rate the object of our interest, and apply to it a language of praise which is quite exaggerated. And thus we get the source of a second fallacy in our poetic judgments-the fallacy caused by an estimate which we may call personal.

All this is brilliantly and tellingly said, but we must plead for a distinction. Everything depends on the reality of a poet's classic character. If he is a dubious classic, let us sift him; if he is a false classic, let us explode him. But if he is a real classic, if his work belongs to the class of the very best (for this is the true and right meaning of the word classic, classical), then the great thing for us is to feel and enjoy his work as deeply as ever we can, and to appreciate the wide difference between it and all work which has not the same high character. This is what is salutary, this is what is formative; this is the great benefit to be got from the study of poetry. Everything which interferes with it, which hinders it, is injurious. True, we must read our classic with open eyes, and not with eyes blinded with superstition; we must perceive when his work comes short, when it drops out of the class of the very best, and we must rate it, in such cases, at its proper value. But the use of this negative criticism is not in itself, it is entirely in its enabling us to have a clearer sense and a deeper enjoyment of what is truly excellent. . .

The idea of tracing historic origins and historical relationships cannot be absent from a compilation like the present. And naturally the poets to be exhibited in it will be assigned to those persons for exhibition who are known to prize them highly, rather than to those who have no special inclination towards them. Moreover the very occupation with an author, and the business of exhibiting him, disposes us to affirm and amplify his importance. In the present work, therefore, we are sure of frequent temptation to adopt the historic estimate, or the personal estimate, and to forget the real estimate; which latter, nevertheless, we must employ if we are to make poetry yield us its full benefit. So high is that benefit, the benefit of clearly feeling and of deeply enjoying the really excellent, the truly classic in poetry, that we do well, I say, to set it fixedly before our minds as our object in studying poets and poetry, and to make the desire of attaining it the one principle to which, as the Imitation says, whatever we may read or come to know, we always return.

The historic estimate is likely in especial to affect our judgment and our language when we are dealing with ancient poets; the personal estimate when we are dealing with poets our contemporaries, or at any rate modern. The exaggerations due to the historic estimate are not in themselves, perhaps, of very much gravity. Their report hardly enters the general ear; probably they do not always impose even on the literary men who adopt them. But they lead to a dangerous abuse of language. . .

Indeed there can be no more useful help for discovering what poetry belongs to the class of the truly excellent, and can therefore do us most good, than to have always in one's mind lines and expressions of the great masters, and to apply them as a touchstone to other poetry. Of course we are not to require this other poetry to resemble them; it may be very dissimilar. But if we have any tact we shall find them, when we have lodged them well in our minds, an infallible touchstone for detecting the presence or absence of high poetic quality, and also the degree of this quality, in all other poetry which we may place beside them. Short passages, even single lines, will serve our turn quite sufficiently. . .

These few lines, if we have tact and can use them, are enough even of themselves to keep clear and sound our judgments about poetry, to save us from fallacious estimates of it, to conduct us to a real estimate. . . . .

The specimens I have quoted differ widely from one another, but they have in common this: the possession of the very highest poetical quality. If we are thoroughly penetrated by their power, we shall find that we have acquired a sense enabling us, whatever poetry may be laid before us, to feel the degree in which a high poetical quality is present or wanting there. Critics give themselves great labor to draw out what in the abstract constitutes the characters of a high quality of poetry. It is much better simply to have recourse to concrete examples; - to take specimens of poetry of the high, the very highest quality, and to say: The characters of a high quality of poetry are what is expressed there. They are far better recognized by being felt in the verse of the master, than by being perused in the prose of the critic.

Nevertheless if we are urgently pressed to give some critical account of them, we may safely, perhaps, venture on laying down, not indeed how and why the characters arise, but where and in what they arise. They are in the matter and substance of the poetry, and they are in its manner and style. Both of these, the substance and matter on the *one hand, the style and manner on the other, have a mark, an accent, of high beauty, worth, and power. But if we are asked to define this mark and accent in the abstract, our answer must be: No, for we should thereby be darkening the question, not clearing it. The mark and accent are as given by the substance and matter of that poetry, by the style and manner of that poetry, and of all other poetry which is akin to it in quality.*

Only one thing we may add as to the substance and matter of poetry, guiding ourselves by Aristotle's profound observation that the superiority of poetry over history consists in its possessing a higher truth and a higher seriousness. Let us add, therefore, to what we have said, this: that the substance and matter of the best poetry acquire their special character from possessing, in an eminent degree, truth and seriousness. We may add yet further, what is in itself evident, that to the style and manner of the best poetry their special character, their accent, is given by their diction, and, even yet more, by their movement. And though we distinguish between the two characters, the two accents, of superiority, yet they are nevertheless vitally connected one with the other. The superior character of truth and seriousness, in the matter and substance of the best poetry, is inseparable from the superiority of diction and movement marking its style and manner. The two superiorities are closely related, and are in steadfast proportion one to the other. So far as high poetic truth and seriousness are wanting to a poet's matter and substance, so far also, we may be sure, will a high poetic stamp of diction and movement be wanting to his style and manner. In proportion as this high stamp of diction and movement, again, is absent from a poet's style and manner, we shall find, also, that high poetic truth and seriousness are absent from his substance and matter. . .

If we ask ourselves wherein consists the immense superiority of Chaucer's poetry over the romance-poetry- why it is that in passing from this to Chaucer we suddenly feel ourselves to be in another world, we shall find that his superiority is both in the substance of his poetry and in the style of his poetry. His superiority in substance is given by his large, free, simple, clear yet kindly view of human life, so unlike the total want, in the romance-poets, of all intelligent command of it. Chaucer has not their helplessness; he has gained the power to survey the world from a central, a truly human point of view. We have only to call to mind the Prologue to The Canterbury Tales. The right comment upon it is Dryden's: "It is sufficient to say, according to the proverb, that here is God's plenty." And again: "He is a perpetual fountain of good sense." It is by a large, free, sound representation of things, that poetry, this high criticism of life, has truth of substance; and Chaucer's poetry has truth of substance. . .

Chaucer is the father of our splendid English poetry; he is our "well of English undefiled," because by the lovely charm of his diction, the lovely charm of his movement, he makes an epoch and founds a tradition. In Spenser, Shakespeare, Milton, Keats, we can follow the tradition of the liquid diction, the fluid movement, of Chaucer; at one time it is his liquid diction of which in these poets we feel the virtue, and at another time it is his fluid movement. And the virtue is irresistible. . .

It is true that Chaucer's fluidity is conjoined with this liberty, and is admirably served by it; but we ought not to say that it was dependent upon it. It was dependent upon his talent. Other poets with a like liberty do not attain to the fluidity of Chaucer; Burns himself does not attain to it. Poets, again, who have a talent akin to Chaucer's, such as Shakespeare or Keats, have known how to attain to his fluidity without the like liberty.

And yet Chaucer is not one of the great classics. And yet, I say, Chaucer is not one of the great classics. He has not their accent. . .However we may account for its absence, something is wanting, then, to the poetry of Chaucer, which poetry must have before it can be placed in the glorious class of the best. And there is no doubt what that something is. It is the high and excellent seriousness, which Aristotle assigns as one of the grand virtues of poetry. The substance of Chaucer's poetry, his view of things and his criticism of life, has largeness, freedom, shrewdness, benignity; but it has not this high seriousness. Homer's criticism of life has it, Dante's has it, and Shakespeare's has it. ...

To our praise, therefore, of Chaucer as a poet there must be this limitation: he lacks the high seriousness of the great classics, and therewith an important part of their virtue. Still, the main fact for us to bear in mind about Chaucer is his sterling value according to that real estimate which we firmly adopt for all poets. He has poetic truth of substance, though he has not high poetic seriousness, and corresponding to his truth of substance he has an exquisite virtue of style and manner. With him is born our real poetry. . .

We are to regard Dryden as the puissant and glorious founder, Pope as the splendid high priest, of our age of prose and reason, of our excellent and indispensable eighteenth century. For the purposes of their mission and destiny their poetry, like their prose, is admirable. Do you ask me whether Dryden's verse, take it almost where you will, is not good?

I answer: Admirable for the purposes of the inaugurator of an age of prose and reason. Do you ask me whether Pope's verse, take it almost where you will, is not good?

I answer: Admirable for the purposes of the high priest of an age of prose and reason. But do you ask me whether such verse proceeds from men with an adequate poetic criticism of life, from men whose criticism of life has a high seriousness, or even, without that high seriousness, has poetic largeness, freedom, insight, benignity? Do you ask me whether the application of ideas to life in the verse of these men, often a powerful application, no doubt, is a powerful poetic application? Do you ask me whether the poetry of these men has either the matter or the inseparable manner of such an adequate poetic criticism; whether it has the accent of "Absent thee from felicity awhile ... " or of "And what is else not to be overcome" or of "O martyr sounded in virginitee!" I answer: It has not and cannot have them; it is the poetry of the builders of an age of prose and reason.

Though they may write in verse, though they may in a certain sense be masters of the art of versification, Dryden and Pope are not classics of our poetry; they are classics of our prose.

Gray is our poetical classic of that literature and age; the position of Gray is singular, and demands a word of notice here. He has not the volume or the power of poets who, coming in times more favorable, have attained to an independent criticism of life. But he lived with the great poets, he lived, above all, with the Greeks, through perpetually studying and enjoying them; and he caught their poetic point of view for regarding life, caught their poetic manner. The point of view and the manner are not self-sprung in him, he caught them of others; and he had not the free and abundant use of them. But whereas Addison and Pope never had the use of them, Gray had the use of them at times. He is the scantiest and frailest of classics in our poetry, but he is a classic. . .

There is a great deal of that sort of thing in Burns, and it is unsatisfactory, not because it is bacchanalian poetry, but because it has not that accent of sincerity which bacchanalian poetry, to do it justice, very often has. There is something in it of bravado, something which makes us feel that we have not the man speaking to us with his real voice: something, therefore, poetically unsound.

There is criticism of life for you, the admirers of Burns will say to us; there is the application of ideas to life! And the application is a powerful one; made by a man of vigorous understanding, and (need I say?) a master of language. . . No; Burns, like Chaucer, comes short of the high seriousness of the great classics, and the virtue of matter and manner which goes with that high seriousness is wanting to his work. . .

But we enter on burning ground as we approach the poetry of times so near to us - poetry like that of Byron, Shelley, and Wordsworth - of which the estimates are so often not only personal, but personal with passion. For my purpose, it is enough to have taken the single case of Burns, the first poet we come to of whose work the estimate formed is evidently apt to be personal, and to have suggested how we may proceed, using the poetry of the great classics as a sort of touchstone, to correct this estimate, as we had previously corrected by the same means the historic estimate where we met with it. A collection like the present, with its succession of celebrated names and celebrated poems, offers a good opportunity to us for resolutely endeavoring to make our estimates of poetry real. I have sought to point out a method which will help us in making them so, and to exhibit it in use so far as to put any one who likes in a way of applying it for himself.

At any rate the end to which the method and the estimate are designed to lead, and from leading to which, if they do lead to it, they get their whole value,- the benefit of being able clearly to feel and deeply to enjoy the best, the truly classic, in poetry,- is an end, let me say it once more at parting, of supreme importance. We are often told that an era is opening in which we are to see multitudes of a common sort of readers, and masses of a common sort of literature; that such readers do not want and could not relish anything better than such literature, and that to provide it is becoming a vast and profitable industry. Even if good literature entirely lost currency with the world, it would still be abundantly worth while to continue to enjoy it by oneself. But it never will lose currency with the world, in spite of momentary appearances; it never will lose supremacy. Currency and supremacy are insured to it, not indeed by the world's deliberate and conscious choice, but by something far deeper, - by the instinct of self-preservation in humanity.

Study Material
1. Summary
(1) In Matthew Arnold's essay "The Study of Poetry," which is perhaps his most famous piece of literary criticism, Arnold is fundamentally concerned with poetry's "high destiny;" he believes that "mankind will discover that we have to turn to poetry to interpret life for us, to console us, to sustain us" as science and philosophy will eventually prove flimsy and unstable. Arnold's essay thus concerns itself with articulating a "high standard" and "strict judgment" in order to avoid the fallacy of valuing certain poems (and poets) too highly, and lays out a method for discerning only the best and therefore "classic" poets (as distinct from the description of writers of the ancient world). Arnold's classic poets include Milton, Shakespeare, Dante, and Homer; and the passages he presents from each are intended to show how their poetry is timeless and moving. For Arnold, feeling and sincerity are paramount, as is the seriousness of subject: "The superior character of truth and seriousness, in the matter and substance of the best poetry, is inseparable from the superiority of diction and movement marking its style and manner." An example of an indispensable poet who falls short of Arnold's "classic" designation is Geoffrey Chaucer, who, Arnold states, ultimately lacks the "high seriousness" of classic poets.

At the root of Arnold's argument is his desire to illuminate and preserve the poets he believes to be the touchstones of literature, and to ask questions about the moral value of poetry that does not champion truth, beauty, valor, and clarity. Arnold's belief that poetry should both uplift and console drives the essay's logic and its conclusions.

(2) In the essay "The Study of Poetry", Arnold attempts a brief comparison between poetry and religion and reaches the conclusion that the dogmatic elements in Christianity are less enduring than the poetic elements. In the age of science when many fundamental principles underlying Christianity are questioned, the traditional faith in Christianity has loosened. This, according to Arnold, would lead the public attention away from religion to poetry. People would turn to

poetry for what religion has been providing them for centuries. Arnold is making an indirect suggestion that the poet's responsibility has increased in the age of science and now it is faced with the task of performing the function of religion. Arnold redefines poetry as "a criticism of life under the conditions fixed for such a criticism by the laws of poetic truth and poetic beauty". His argument is that when dogmatic religions failed to provide ethical and spiritual consolation to people, poetry will have to be a source of consolation and comfort. For that poetry has to become serious and it can perform this function only to the extent to which it remains a criticism of life.

After assigning a serious social function to poetry Arnold says that only poetry of high excellence will be able to perform its vital social function. The reader should know what is good poetry and hear lies the crucial role of the critic. Arnold is critical of the existing methods by which poets are judged; the two common methods- 'Historic estimate' and 'Personal estimate' are, according to him, fallacious. Arnold then proposes a new method of evaluating poetry. He suggests that we should have in our mind lines and expressions of the great masters of poetry, and that we should apply them as a touchstone to other poetry. He writes, "Of course we are not to require this other poetry to resemble them; it may be very dissimilar. But if we have any tact we shall find them, when we have locked them well in our minds, an infallible touchstone for detecting the presence or absence of high poetic quality, and also the degree of this quality, in all other poetry which we may place beside them." By taking a few passages from Homer, Dante, Shakespeare and Milton, he points out how they impress alike by their poetical quality. So they all 'belong to the class of the truly excellent'. He concludes, "Critics give themselves great lobour to draw out what in the abstract constitutes the characters of a high quality of poetry. It is much better simply to have recourse to concrete examples; - to take specimens of poetry of the high, the very high quality, and to say: the characters of high quality of poetry are what is expressed there. They are far better recognized by being felt in the verse of the master, than by being pursued in the prose of the critic." Arnold is unable to suggest any concrete criterion by which these 'characters of a high quality of poetry' may be determined; he considers 'tact' or taste as sure enough guide. According to Arnold, the qualities of the highest kind of poetry can be found in the matter of poetry and also in its manner and style. In connection with matter and style of poetry Arnold is guided by the Aristotelian notion that the superiority of poetry over history consists in its possessing a higher truth and seriousness. Arnold says, "The best poetry is characterized by truth and seriousness to an eminent degree." As regards the manner and style, "the best poetry is characterized by the superiority of diction and of movement." In his view the two 'superiorities' are closely related, and are in steadfast proportion to each other. So far as high poetic truth and seriousness are wanting in a poet's matter and substance, so far also will a high poetic stamp of diction and movement be wanting in his style and manner.

2. A Critical Assessment of Arnold's Essay

Literary Criticism, as Matthew Arnold (1822-1888), the Victorian poet and critic points out, is a "disinterested endeavor to learn and propagate" the best that is known and thought in the world. And he strove hard to fulfill this aim in his critical writings. Attaching paramount importance to poetry in his essay "The Study of Poetry", he regards the poet as seer. Without poetry, science is incomplete, and much of religion and philosophy would in future be replaced by poetry. Such, in his estimate, are the high destinies of poetry.

Arnold asserts that literature, and especially poetry, is "Criticism of Life". In poetry, this criticism of life must conform to the laws of poetic truth and poetic beauty. Truth and seriousness of matter, felicity and perfection of diction and manner, as are exhibited in the best poets, are what constitutes a criticism of life.

Poetry, says Arnold, interprets life in two ways: "Poetry is interpretative by having natural magic in it, and moral profundity". And to achieve this, the poet must aim at high and excellent seriousness in all that he writes. This demand has two essential qualities. The first is the choice of excellent actions. The poet must choose those which most powerfully appeal to the great primary human feelings which subsist permanently in the race. The second essential is what Arnold calls the Grand Style - the perfection of form, choice of words, drawing its force directly from the pregnancy of matter which it conveys.

This, then, is Arnold's conception of the nature and mission of true poetry. And by his general principles - the" Touchstone Method" - introduced scientific objectivity to critical evaluation by providing comparison and analysis as the two primary tools for judging individual poets. Thus, Chaucer, Dryden, Pope, and Shelley fall short of the best, because they lack "high seriousness". Even Shakespeare thinks too much of expression and too little of conception. Arnold's ideal poets are Homer and Sophocles in the ancient world, Dante and Milton, and among moderns, Goethe and Wordsworth. Arnold puts Wordsworth in the front rank not for his poetry but for his "criticism of life". It is curious that Byron is placed above Shelley. Arnold's inordinate love of classicism made him blind to the beauty of lyricism, and we cannot accept Arnold's view that Shelley's poetry is less satisfactory than his prose writings.

In 'The Study of Poetry' Matthew Arnold has presented poetry as a criticism of life. In the beginning of his essay he states: "In poetry as criticism of life, under conditions fixed for such criticism by the laws of poetic truth and poetic beauty, the spirit of our race will find, as time goes by and as other helps fail, its consolation and stay." Thus, according to him poetry is governed by the laws of poetic truth and poetic beauty.

Poetic truth is a characteristic quality of the matter and substance of poetry. It means a sound representation of life. In other words, it is a true depiction of life without any attempt to falsify the facts. Poetic beauty is contained in the manner and style. It is marked by excellence of diction and flow of verse. While talking of Chaucer, Arnold mentions fluidity of diction and verse. Poetic beauty springs from right words in the right order.

Poetic truth and poetic beauty are inter-related and cannot be separated from one another." The superior character of truth and seriousness in the matter and substance of best poetry, is inseparable from the superiority of diction and movement marking its manner and style", says Arnold. If a poem is lacking in the qualities of poetic truth and high seriousness, it cannot possess the excellence of diction and movement, and vice-versa.

In his estimate of Burns and Wordsworth, Arnold points out that another characteristic of great poetry is application of ideas to criticism of life. The greatness of Wordsworth lies in his powerful application of the subject of ideas to man, nature and human life. Ideas according to Arnold are moral ideas.

Another quality attributed to great poetry by Arnold is that of 'high seriousness'. Although he does not fully explain the term, we gather quite a lot of information from his statement. Aristotle was of the view that poetry is superior to History due to the former's qualities of higher truth and higher seriousness. What we judge from Arnold's essay is that high-seriousness is concerned with the sad reality. This quality is possessed by poetry which deals with the tragic aspects of life. Even the examples given by Arnold from Dante, Shakespeare and Milton's poetry illustrate this view.

Regarding the concept of criticism of life, it needs to be understood what Arnold meant by the phrase - "criticism of life". It does not mean carping at or unnecessarily finding faults with life. The suggestion itself is unsound that it means a criticism of society and its follies. Criticism of life means a healthy interpretation of life. It means an evaluation, sympathetic sharing in and feeling for. The theory of poetry given Arnold has been challenged on many accounts. Arnold does not consider Burns a great poet because in his poetry Burns presents an ugly life. Arnold was of the view that a poet has the advantage of portraying a beautiful life in his poetry. Eliot attacked this opinion. He believed that the poet has not the advantage of describing a beautiful life but has rather an advantage of having the capacity to look beneath both ugliness and beauty. It is the power to look beyond boredom, horror and glory.

While teaching of the concept of poetic beauty, Arnold mentions excellence of diction but does not explain what it is. As regards the flow in verse or the fluidity in movement, Arnold probably does not realize that the use of coarseness is sometimes intentional to create a specific effect. Smoothness need not be the only one; harshness and ruggedness are equally great qualities, when used to create special effects.

Matthew Arnold does not fully explain the term 'high seriousness'. It should also be remembered here that seriousness should not at all be considered synonymous with solemnity. The serious and humorous can exist together.

Another view put forward by Arnold that has been under the shadow of criticism is that of 'ideas'. We might very well like to believe that what Arnold wants to say is that an author, while interpreting life for us, might also use a moral idea to convey a moral lesson. But what Arnold believes is that there is a pre-conceived idea on which the poet bases his evaluation.

Eliot also criticizes Arnold on the latter's occupation with only great poetry. Adhering to this principle, we might end up dealing with only a small part of the total poetry.

Matthew Arnold talks of deriving pleasure from poetry. But according to critics he is actually biased towards morality - a fact that is evident from his view that poetry would replace religion. "More and more mankind will discover that we have to turn to poetry to interpret life for us", he writes.

Apart from all the negative criticism directed against Arnold we cannot deny that he has very beautifully related literature to life. As Douglas Bush rightly points out that literature is not an end in itself for Arnold. It only adds to the beauty of life and answers the question 'How to live?' Arnold is such a person, who does not live to read, but reads to live.

(5) T.S.Eliot : *Tradition and the Individual Talent*

In 1919 T. S. Eliot wrote the world famous essay 'Tradition and Individual Talent', a very potent essay pregnant with many concepts, among them poetry and tradition being the major one. His concept of poetry was primarily an attack on the romantic concept of poetry especially Eliot attacked Wordsworth's famous concept "Poetry is spontaneous overflow of powerful feelings: it takes its origin from emotions recollected in tranquillity". Eliot was completely against this romantic concept of poetry because for him poetry is not recollection of feeling but poetry is a new thing resulting from the concentration of a very great number of experiences and for Eliot this concentration does not happen consciously or deliberately. For Eliot "poetry is not a turning loose of emotions, but an escape from emotions, it is not the expression of the personality but an escape from personality. For romantics poetry was expression of personality of the poet but Eliot believed that the personal experiences important for a man may not have any place in his poems. He firmly believed that the personal life and personal emotions however important may not be important for the poet, as a poet. For Eliot what matters is emotions transmuted in the poem feelings expressed in the poetry. For Eliot the emotion of art is impersonal and dispassionate and the artist can achieve this impersonality only by cultivating the historical sense and by being conscious of the traditions.

For Eliot the poet must merge his personality with tradition, in this essay he says that "the progress of the artist is the continual self sacrifice, a continual extinction of personality". For Eliot mind of a poet is a medium in which experiences can enter into new combinations that is why he says that poet is a catalyst and poet's mind is a 'receptacle' which holds numberless feelings images, phrases and emotions. The combination of that in a particular form is art or poetry. Thus, the poetic process is a process of depersonalization, impersonalization or extinction of personality not what the romantics' propagated expression of personality.

For Eliot, tradition is one of the main concept and necessity for the poet or artist to be a creator. Tradition for Eliot means an awareness of the history of Europe, not as a dead facts and dates but as "as an ever changing yet changeless presence." The constantly interacting subconscious element of the point. The poet must not forget the 'mind of Europe', he is not only a mind but a part of greater continent. Eliot's idea of tradition can be understood on two levels, first, the simple meaning of poetic tradition in which the socio-political and historical presence of poetry in the oral and written forms of poetry is included. Second, tradition for him as a non-poetic element in which the social and economical formulations affect the ideological frame work in which it takes place. For Eliot, tradition includes culture, history and literature, religion, polity and morality are also included, he firmly believed that tradition is more larger and expansive than culture. Eliot sees this literary tradition as a construct of the collective-historical unconscious. It is because of this sense of timelessness that poetry is at once a product of tradition and a product of its own time. To Eliot literary tradition is a living, growing, and ever changing organism which poetic genius taps into and draws from in order to create a new work, which may in turn become a new part of the living whole.

In short, this essay pioneers the new understandings of poetry, talent, tradition and even criticism. This essay heralded 'The New Criticism', The Chicago School of Criticism', and 'The Practical Criticism'. At the base of The Modern aesthetic and critical practises is Eliot's concept of poetry and tradition in this essay 'Tradition and Individual Talent'.

Tradition and the Individual Talent (1919)
(The Text)

In English writing we seldom speak of tradition, though we occasionally apply its name in deploring its absence. We cannot refer to "the tradition" or to "a tradition"; at most, we employ the adjective in saying that the poetry of So-and-so is "traditional" or even "too traditional." Seldom, perhaps, does the word appear except in a phrase of censure. . .

Certainly the word is not likely to appear in our appreciations of living or dead writers. Every nation, every race, has not only its own creative, but its own critical turn of mind; and is even more oblivious of the shortcomings and limitations of its critical habits than of those of its creative genius. We know, or think we know, from the enormous mass of critical writing that has appeared in the French language the critical method or habit of the French; we only conclude (we are such unconscious people) that the French are "more critical" than we, and sometimes even plume ourselves a little with the fact, as if the French were the less spontaneous. Perhaps they are; but we might remind ourselves that criticism is as inevitable as breathing, and that we should be none the worse for articulating what passes in our minds when we read a book and feel an emotion about it, for criticizing our own minds in their work of criticism. One of the facts that might come to light in this process is our tendency to insist, when we praise a poet, upon those aspects of his work in which he least resembles anyone else. In these aspects or parts of his work we pretend to find what is individual, what is the peculiar essence of the man. We dwell with satisfaction upon the poet's difference from his predecessors, especially his immediate predecessors; we endeavour to find something that can be isolated in order to be enjoyed. Whereas if we approach a poet without this prejudice we shall often find that not only the best, but the most individual parts of his work may be those in which the dead poets, his ancestors, assert their immortality most vigorously. And I do not mean the impressionable period of adolescence, but the period of full maturity.

Yet if the only form of tradition, of handing down, consisted in following the ways of the immediate generation before us in a blind or timid adherence to its successes, "tradition" should positively be discouraged. We have seen many such simple currents soon lost in the *sand; and novelty is better than repetition. Tradition is a matter of much wider significance. It cannot be inherited, and if you want it you must obtain it by great labour. It involves, in the first place, the historical sense, which we may call nearly indispensable to anyone who would continue to be a poet beyond his twenty-fifth year; and the historical sense involves a perception, not only of the pastness of the past, but of its presence; the historical sense compels a man to write not merely with his own generation in his bones, but with a feeling that the whole of the literature of Europe from Homer and within it the whole of the literature of his own country has a simultaneous existence and composes a simultaneous order. This historical sense, which is a sense of the timeless as well as of the temporal and of the timeless and of the temporal together, is what makes a writer traditional. And it is at the same time what makes a writer most acutely conscious of his place in time, of his contemporaneity.*

No poet, no artist of any art, has his complete meaning alone. His significance, his appreciation is the appreciation of his relation to the dead poets and artists. You cannot value him alone; you must set him, for contrast and comparison, among the dead. I mean this as a principle of æsthetic, not merely historical, criticism. The necessity that he shall conform, that he shall cohere, is not one-sided; what happens when a new work of art is created is something that happens simultaneously to all the works of art which preceded it. The existing monuments form an ideal order among themselves, which is modified by the introduction of the new (the really new) work of art among them. The existing order is complete before the new work arrives; for order to persist after the supervention of novelty, the whole existing order must be, if ever so slightly, altered; and so the relations, proportions, values of each work of art toward the whole are readjusted; and this is conformity between the old and the new. Whoever has approved this idea of order, of the form of European, of English literature, will not find it preposterous that the past should be altered by the present as much as the present is directed by the past. And the poet who is aware of this will be aware of great difficulties and responsibilities.

In a peculiar sense he will be aware also that he must inevitably be judged by the standards of the past. I say judged, not amputated, by them; not judged to be as good as, or worse or better than, the dead; and certainly not judged by the canons of dead critics. It is a judgment, a comparison, in which two things are measured by each other. To conform merely would be for the new work not really to conform at all; it would not be new, and would therefore not be a work of art. And we do not quite say that the new is more valuable because it fits in; but its fitting in is a test of its value- a test, it is true, which can only be slowly and cautiously applied, for we are none of us infallible judges of conformity. We say: it appears to conform, and is perhaps individual, or it appears individual, and may conform; but we are hardly likely to find that it is one and not the other.

To proceed to a more intelligible exposition of the relation of the poet to the past: he can neither take the past as a lump, an indiscriminate bolus, nor can he form himself wholly on one or two private admirations, nor can he form himself wholly upon one preferred period. The first course is inadmissible, the second is an important experience of youth, and the third is a pleasant and highly desirable supplement. The poet must be very conscious of the main current, which does not at all flow invariably through the most distinguished reputations. He must be quite aware of the obvious fact that art never improves, but that the material of art is never quite the same. He must be aware that the mind of Europe—the mind of his own country—a mind which he learns in time to be much more important than his own private mind—is a mind which changes, and that this change is a development which abandons nothing en route, which does not superannuate either Shakespeare, or Homer, or the rock drawing of the Magdalenian draughtsmen. That this development, refinement perhaps, complication certainly, is not, from the point of view of the artist, any improvement. Perhaps not even an improvement from the point of view of the psychologist or not to the extent which we imagine; perhaps only in the end based upon a complication in economics and machinery. But the difference between the present and the past is that the conscious present is an awareness of the past in a way and to an extent which the past's awareness of itself cannot show.

Some one said: "The dead writers are remote from us because we know so much more than they did." Precisely, and they are that which we know. ...

What happens is a continual surrender of himself as he is at the moment to something which is more valuable. The progress of an artist is a continual self-sacrifice, a continual extinction of personality.

There remains to define this process of depersonalization and its relation to the sense of tradition. It is in this depersonalization that art may be said to approach the condition of science. I shall, therefore, invite you to consider, as a suggestive analogy, the action which takes place when a bit of finely filiated platinum is introduced into a chamber containing oxygen and sulphur dioxide.

II

... The analogy was that of the catalyst. When the two gases previously mentioned are mixed in the presence of a filament of platinum, they form sulphurous acid. This combination takes place only if the platinum is present; nevertheless the newly formed acid contains no trace of platinum, and the platinum itself is apparently unaffected; has remained inert, neutral, and unchanged. The mind of the poet is the shred of platinum. It may partly or exclusively operate upon the experience of the man himself; but, the more perfect the artist, the more completely separate in him will be the man who suffers and the mind which creates; the more perfectly will the mind digest and transmute the passions which are its material.

The experience, you will notice, the elements which enter the presence of the transforming catalyst, are of two kinds: emotions and feelings. The effect of a work of art upon the person who enjoys it is an experience different in kind from any experience not of art. It may be formed out of one emotion, or may be a combination of several; and various feelings, inhering for the writer in particular words or phrases or images, may be added to compose the final result. Or great poetry may be made without the direct use of any emotion whatever: composed out of feelings solely. ... The poet's mind is in fact a receptacle for seizing and storing up numberless feelings, phrases, images, which remain there until all the particles which can unite to form a new compound are present together.

If you compare several representative passages of the greatest poetry you see how great is the variety of types of combination, and also how completely any semi-ethical criterion of "sublimity" misses the mark. For it is not the "greatness," the intensity, of the emotions, the components, but the intensity of the artistic process, the pressure, so to speak, under which the fusion takes place, that counts. ... The ode

*of Keats contains a number of feelings which have nothing particular
to do with the nightingale, but which the nightingale, partly, perhaps,
because of its attractive name, and partly because of its reputation,
served to bring together.*

*The point of view which I am struggling to attack is perhaps
related to the metaphysical theory of the substantial unity of the soul:
for my meaning is, that the poet has, not a "personality" to express,
but a particular medium, which is only a medium and not a personality,
in which impressions and experiences combine in peculiar and
unexpected ways. Impressions and experiences which are important
for the man may take no place in the poetry, and those which become
important in the poetry may play quite a negligible part in the man, the
personality. ...*

*It is not in his personal emotions, the emotions provoked by
particular events in his life, that the poet is in any way remarkable or
interesting. His particular emotions may be simple, or crude, or flat.
The emotion in his poetry will be a very complex thing, but not with the
complexity of the emotions of people who have very complex or unusual
emotions in life. One error, in fact, of eccentricity in poetry is to seek
for new human emotions to express; and in this search for novelty in
the wrong place it discovers the perverse. The business of the poet is
not to find new emotions, but to use the ordinary ones and, in working
them up into poetry, to express feelings which are not in actual emotions
at all. And emotions which he has never experienced will serve his turn
as well as those familiar to him. Consequently, we must believe that
"emotion recollected in tranquillity" is an inexact formula. For it is
neither emotion, nor recollection, nor, without distortion of meaning,
tranquillity. It is a concentration, and a new thing resulting from the
concentration, of a very great number of experiences which to the
practical and active person would not seem to be experiences at all; it
is a concentration which does not happen consciously or of deliberation.
These experiences are not "recollected," and they finally unite in an
atmosphere which is "tranquil" only in that it is a passive attending
upon the event. Of course this is not quite the whole story. There is a
great deal, in the writing of poetry, which must be conscious and
deliberate. In fact, the bad poet is usually unconscious where he ought
to be conscious, and conscious where he ought to be unconscious. Both
errors tend to make him "personal." Poetry is not a turning loose of*

emotion, but an escape from emotion; it is not the expression of personality, but an escape from personality. But, of course, only those who have personality and emotions know what it means to want to escape from these things.

III

"The mind is doubtless more divine and less subject to passion," Aristotle

This essay proposes to halt at the frontier of metaphysics or mysticism, and confine itself to such practical conclusions as can be applied by the responsible person interested in poetry. To divert interest from the poet to the poetry is a laudable aim: for it would conduce to a juster estimation of actual poetry, good and bad. There are many people who appreciate the expression of sincere emotion in verse, and there is a smaller number of people who can appreciate technical excellence. But very few know when there is expression of significant emotion, emotion which has its life in the poem and not in the history of the poet. The emotion of art is impersonal. And the poet cannot reach this impersonality without surrendering himself wholly to the work to be done. And he is not likely to know what is to be done unless he lives in what is not merely the present, but the present moment of the past, unless he is conscious, not of what is dead, but of what is already living.

Study Material
1. Brief Summary

Tradition and the Individual Talent re-values the idea of tradition: in the mature poet past poetry is part of his individuality; the past is part of the present, and is modified by it. Thus what is genuinely new is to be aware of, and a part of, the ever-changing 'mind of Europe.'

To achieve this integral relation with the body of European poetry, a poet must aim at the extinction of his personality. He must be not a personality but a medium for the digestion and transmutation of his material. The result is its own kind of thing; its complexity is not that of the emotion represented or suffered by the man who wrote the poem. Consequently the romantic docrines are rejected as too personal, too crudely related to the emotions of the poet. ... The business of the poem is 'emotion which has its life in the poem,' not the poet's emotions or his opinions. That is why he must strive for Impersonality.

2. Explication of Eliot's Concept of 'Tradition'

Eliot's epoch-making essay of 1919 "Tradition and The Individual Talent" may be considered his official manifesto in which most of his critical principles he developed in later writing were initiated. Eliot lays down in it the basic principles of objectivity and impersonality in poetry. No other critical essay of the 20th century has been as influential as "Tradition and Individual Talent." The essay by no means is easy to read. Let us try to simplify it in order to understand the exact import of what Eliot means to say in this essay.

The word 'tradition' is used by Eliot in a wider sense; it certainly does not restrict itself to literary tradition, (though it is very much a part of it) it refers to social, historical, political, economic, cultural and even ideological tradition-all that exists around us consciously and unconsciously and continues to influence us (even condition us). It is not merely handed down to us. Eliot explains its wider significance as follows:

"It cannot be inherited, and if you want it you must be obtain it by great labour. It involves, in the first place, the historical sense... and the historical sense involves the perception, not only the pastness of the past, but of its presence; the historical sense compels a man to write not merely with his own generation in his bones, but with the feeling that the whole of the literature of Europe from Homer and within it the whole of the literature of his own country has a simultaneous existence and composes a simultaneous order.

Eliot is clarifying here the relationship between tradition and the individual talent of a writer. A good and significant writer becomes aware, through the historical sense, of tradition, being formed jointly by the old and the new. It is therefore (without any article) just 'tradition.' Such tradition is ever- changing and the individual talent of a writer modifies it, when a new work arrives. A writer is related to other writers of the past. So Eliot says, no poet has his complete meaning alone. The relation between tradition and the talent enables the past to be altered by the present, as much as the present is directed by the past.

For Eliot tradition does not mean anything fixed. A writer with talent picks up and chooses the writer/s, the age, the modes, the literary structures that he considers significant for his own works. Eliot's own sense of tradition rejected the Romantics in favour of the Metaphysical, the Elizabethans and the Jacobeans, but that was what Eliot the poet preferred to be his tradition. Every literary talent, according to Eliot's theory, has this freedom to be traditional in his own way. But in order to be so traditional, a talent has to give up being personal, he has to become impersonal. So the last sentences of the first section of the essay run as follows: "What happens is a continual surrender of himself as he is at the moment to something which is more valuable. The progress of an artist is a continual self- sacrifice, a continual extinction of personality."

The second section of the essay tries to elucidate Eliot's theory of impersonality. He says, "The poet has, not a personality to express, but a particular medium, which is only a medium and not a personality, in which impressions and experiences combined in peculiar and unexpected ways." And so here comes the difficulty of the essay. Eliot uses the analogy of the catalyst. The mind of the great poet is like the shred of platinum, in a chemical process. One can present the chemical equation as follows :

$$2SO_2 \ + \ O_2 \ \xrightarrow[\text{Catalyst}]{\text{Platinum}} \ 2SO_3$$

Sulphur + Oxygen dioxide   Sulphur trioxide

Many readers and critics of Eliot were led to be believe that Eliot was equating the creative process with a chemical process. Most of them forgot that Eliot was using an analogy, a metaphor from chemistry. (This is probably the second striking use of a metaphor by a western literary critic to explain a complex process: the first was the metaphor of 'Catharsis' used by Aristotle to explain the nature of tragic pleasure). Once this is understood, Eliot's statement becomes quite clear when he says: (i) "the more perfect the artist, the more completely separate in him will be the man who suffers and the mind which creates." (ii) "Poetry is not a turning loose of emotion, but an escape from emotion; it is not the expression of personality, but an escape from personality." (iii) "The emotion of art is impersonal."

Eliot's concept of tradition and his theory of impersonality can be understood by visualizing the creative process he has gone through in writing *The Waste Land,* the most representative poetic achievement of the twentieth century.

To sum up, Eliot is undoubtedly the most influential of all modern critics. He is a classicist directly in the line of Aristotle. As a critic, Eliot taught how to look steadfastly at the object to arrive at the precise definition of it. Endowed with a scientific mind, wholly devoted to inquiry, Eliot not only talked about critical principles, but also practiced them successfully. Eliot's criticism is highly original and thought provoking. In throwing light on a number of writers and their works, Eliot has rendered a great service to literature by reforming taste and revitalizing literature. No doubt, he is the fountainhead of most of the critical ideas of his age.

❏❏

4
Literary and Critical Concepts & Terms

A few literary terms and critical concepts are discussed below. An attempt is made to present the essence of the concept along with some additional explanation. It should be remembered that a reader has to make extra efforts to support the explanation given here in order to grasp the concepts and ideas therein.

(1) Allusion

An allusion is a brief reference in a written work to a person, event, place, a phrase, a myth, an idea in history or another artistic work. The writer generally assumes will recognize the reference. The nature and relevance of allusion is not explained by the writer but relies on the reader's familiarity with what is thus mentioned. The technique of allusion is an economical means of calling upon the history or the literary tradition that author and reader are assumed to share, although some poets (notably Ezra Pound and T. S. Eliot) allude to areas of quite specialized knowledge. In his poem *'The Statues'*-

When Pearse summoned Cuchulain to his side
What stalked through the Post Office?

-W. B. Yeats *alludes* both to the hero of Celtic legend (Cuchulain) and to the new historical hero (Patrick Pearse) of the 1916 Easter Rising, in which the revolutionaries captured the Dublin Post Office. In addition to such *topical* allusions to recent events, Yeats often uses *personal* allusions to aspects of his own life and circle of friends. Other kinds of allusion include the *imitative* and the *structural*, in which one work reminds us of the structure of another (as Joyce's *Ulysses* refers to Homer's *Odyssey*). Topical allusions are especially important in satire.

Allude and *allusion* are often used where the more general terms *refer* and *reference* would be preferable. Normally, both a*llude* and *allusion* apply to indirect references in which the source is not specifically identified. *Refer* and *reference,* unless qualified, usually imply specific mention of a source: *I will refer to* Hamlet *for my conclusion: As Polonius says, "Though this be madness, yet there is method in it."*

Allusion could also be a reference in one literary work to a character or theme found in another literary work. T. S. Eliot, in *The Love Song of J. Alfred Prufrock* alludes to the biblical figure John the Baptist in the line,

Though I have seen my head (grown slightly bald) brought in upon a platter . . .

In the New Testament, John the Baptist's head was presented to King Herod on a platter.

An allusion is a literary device that stimulates ideas, associations, and extra information in the reader's mind with only a word or two. Allusion means 'reference'. It relies on the reader being able to understand the allusion and being familiar with all of the meaning hidden behind the words.

Let us therefore define the term for convenience. An allusion is a reference, within a literary work, to another work of fiction, a film, a piece of art, or even a real event. An allusion serves as a kind of shorthand, drawing on this outside work to provide greater context or meaning to the situation being written about. While allusions can be an economical way of communicating with the reader, they risk alienating readers who do not recognize these references. M.H. Abrams defined allusion as "a brief reference, explicit or indirect, to a person, place or event, or to another literary work or passage." It is left to the reader or hearer to make the connection; therefore an *overt allusion* is a misnomer for what is simply a reference.

Imaginative literature, particularly poetry, often relies on allusions so that the fiction works on both levels. Readers who get the allusions gain a richer understanding of the work, but those who don't can still follow the story and be entertained or enlightened by it. Allusions can be looked upon as a kind of hypertext, linking the reader to another tradition or literary history. For example, T.S. Eliot's "The Wasteland," relies heavily on allusions; for those without a strong classical education, it can be a challenging poem. The poetry of Eliot is often described as "allusive", because of his habit of referring to names, places or images that may only make sense in the light of prior knowledge. This technique can add to the experience, but for the uninitiated can make Eliot's work seem dense and hard to decipher. However, allusions can also be quite subtle. For instance, Shakespeare's influence on literature in English is so strong that we often make allusions to his plays without being aware of it.

Allusions can originate in mythology, biblical references, historical events, legends, geography, or earlier literary works. Authors often use allusion to establish a tone, create an implied association, contrast two objects or people, make an unusual juxtaposition of references, or bring the reader into a world of experience outside the limitations of the story itself. Allusions conjure up biblical authority, scenes from Shakespeare's plays, historic figures, wars, great love stories, and anything else that might enrich an author's work. Allusions imply reading and cultural experiences shared by the writer and reader, functioning as a kind of shorthand whereby the recalling of something outside the work supplies an emotional or intellectual context. Allusions, in contemporary critical theory, are considered under the tern 'Intertextuality.' All great writing includes other works into its own text through intertextuality. Therefore one can say that allusions have become an integral part of all types of literary writing today.

(2) Ambiguity, Connotation and Denotation
Ambiguity

Ambiguity is found in a statement which can contain two or more meanings. For example, when the oracle at Delphi told Croesus that if he waged war on Cyrus he would destroy a great empire, Croesus thought the oracle meant his enemy's empire. In fact, by going to war Croesus destroyed his own empire.

In this sense, ambiguity Allows for two or more simultaneous interpretations of a word, phrase, action, or situation, all of which can be supported by the context of a work. Deliberate ambiguity can contribute to the effectiveness and richness of a work, for example, in the open-ended conclusion to Hawthorne's "Young Goodman Brown." However, unintentional ambiguity obscures meaning and can confuse readers.

Ambiguity exists in a statement whose meaning is unclear. Depending on the circumstances, ambiguity can be negative, leading to confusion or even disaster (the ambiguous wording of a general's note led to the deadly charge of the Light Brigade in the Crimean War). On the other hand, writers often use it to achieve special effects, for instance, to reflect the complexity of an issue or to indicate the difficulty, perhaps the impossibility, of determining truth.

The title of the country song "Heaven's Just a Sin Away" is deliberately ambiguous; at a religious level, it means that committing a sin keeps us out of heaven, but at a physical level, it means that committing a sin (sex) will bring heaven (pleasure). Many of Hamlet's statements to the King, to his friends Rosenkrantz and Guildenstern, and to other characters are deliberately ambiguous, to hide his real purpose from them.

In this context, William Empson's famous book Seven Types of Ambiguity which discusses ambiguity in poetry is worth mentioning. Empson's special contribution in this work was his suggestion that uncertainty or the overlap of meanings in the use of a word could be an enrichment of poetry rather than a fault. Empson uses the term ambiguity 'in an extended sense', to refer to 'any verbal nuance, however slight, which gives room for alternative reactions to the same piece of language' An ambiguity is represented as a puzzle to Empson. We have ambiguity when "alternative views might be taken without sheer misreading." Empson reads poetry as an exploration of conflicts within the author.

Denotation and Connotation

There are two types of meanings of a word: denotation and connotation. One could call the former the basic meaning and the latter the extended meaning. Denotation refers to the minimal, strict definition of a word as found in a dictionary, disregarding any historical or emotional connotation. Denotation, therefore, is the literal meaning of a word; there are no emotions, values, or images associated with denotative meaning. Scientific and mathematical language carries few, if any emotional or connotative meanings. The use of dictionary is mainly for looking up denotations of words.

As against it, Connotation of a word includes the emotions, values, or images associated with it. The intensity of emotions or the power of the values and images associated with a word varies. Words connected with religion, politics, and sex tend to have the strongest feelings and images associated with them. For most people, the word *mother* calls up very strong positive feelings and associations- loving, self-sacrificing, always there for you, understanding; the denotative meaning, on the other hand, is simply "a female animal who has borne one or more children." Of course connotative meanings do not necessarily reflect reality; for instance, if someone said, "His mother is not very motherly," you would immediately understand the difference between *motherly* (connotation) and *mother* (denotation).

Connotation refers to the extra tinge or taint of meaning each word carries beyond the minimal, strict definition found in a dictionary. For instance, the terms *civil war*, *revolution* and *rebellion* have the same denotation; they all refer to an attempt at social or political change. However, *civil war* carries historical connotations for Americans beyond that of *revolution* or *rebellion*. Likewise, *revolution* is often applied more generally to scientific or theoretical changes, and it does not necessarily connote violence. *Rebellion*, for many English speakers connotes an improper uprising against a legitimate authority (thus we speak about "rebellious teenagers" rather than "revolutionary teenagers"). In the same way, the words *house* and *home* both refer to a domicile, but *home* connotes certain singular emotional qualities and personal possession in a way that *house* doesn't. I might own four *houses* I rent to others, but I might call none of these my *home*, for example. Much of poetry involves the poet using connotative diction that suggests meanings beyond "what the words simply say."

(3) Simile, Metaphor, Onomatopoeia, Symbol, Imagery, Conceit

The literary terms used in this section cannot be described using a blanket term. But we can say that simile, metaphor, imagery and conceit, in a general way, refer to figures of speech based on similarity and comparison between dissimilar objects and ideas.

Simile

Simile is a figure of speech which takes the form of a comparison between two unlike quantities for which a basis for comparison can be found, and which uses the words "like" or "as" in the comparison, as in this line from Ezra Pound's "Fan-Piece, for Her Imperial Lord": "clear as frost on the grass-blade." In this line, a fan of white silk is being compared to frost on a blade of grass. Note the use of the word "as." There are so many examples of similes in poetry. Eliot's unusual simile in Love Song of J. Alfred Prufrock surprises, even shocks, the readers: "When the evening is spread out against the sky/ Like a patient etherized upon a table." Robert Burns is famous for his simile in the lines: "My love is like a red red rose/ That's newly sprung in June."

Metaphor

Metaphor is a figure of speech wherein a comparison is made between two unlike quantities without the use of the words "like" or "as." Jonathan Edwards, in his sermon "Sinners in the Hands of an Angry God," has this to say about the moral condition of his parishioners: "There are the black clouds of God's wrath/ Now hanging directly over your heads,/ Full of the dreadful storm and big with thunder." The comparison here is between God's anger and a storm. Note that there is no use of "like" or "as" as would be the case in a simile.

Metaphors thus assert the identity of dissimilar things, as when Macbeth asserts that life is a "brief candle." Metaphors can be subtle and powerful, and can transform people, places, objects, and ideas into whatever the writer imagines them to be. However, metaphors can take different forms. For example, an implied metaphor is a more subtle comparison; the terms being compared are not so specifically explained. For example, to describe a stubborn man unwilling to leave, one could say that he was "a mule standing his ground." This is a fairly explicit metaphor; the man is being compared to a mule. But to say that the man "brayed his refusal to leave" is to create an implied metaphor, because the subject (the man) is never overtly identified as a mule. Braying is associated with the mule, a notoriously stubborn creature, and so the comparison between the stubborn man and the mule is sustained. Implied metaphors can slip by inattentive readers who are not sensitive to such carefully chosen, highly concentrated language. An extended metaphor is a sustained comparison in which part or all of a poem consists of a series of related metaphors. Robert Francis's poem "Catch" relies on an extended metaphor that compares poetry to playing catch. A controlling metaphor runs through an entire work and determines the form or nature of that work. The controlling metaphor in Anne Bradstreet's poem "The Author to Her Book" likens her book to a child. Synecdoche is a kind of metaphor in which a part of something is used to signify the whole, as when a gossip is called a "wagging tongue," or when ten ships are called "ten sails." Sometimes, synecdoche refers to the whole being used to signify the part, as in the phrase "Boston won the baseball game." Clearly, the entire city of Boston did not participate in the game; the whole of Boston is being used to signify the individuals who played and won the game. Metonymy is a type of metaphor in which something closely associated with a subject is substituted for it. In this way, we speak of the "silver screen" to mean motion pictures, "the crown" to stand for the king, "the White House" to stand for the activities of the president.

Onomatopoeia

Onomatopoeia is a word that imitates or suggests the source of the sound that it describes. Onomatopoeia refers to the property of such words. Common occurrences of onomatopoeias include animal noises, such as "meow" or "roar". Onomatopoeias are not universally the same across all languages; they conform to some extent to the broader linguistic system they are part of; hence the sound of a clock may be *tick tock* in English and *tik tak* in Dutch or *tic-tac* in French and *tick tick* in Marathi.

Some other very common English-language examples include *hiccup, zoom, bang, beep,* and *splash*. Machines and their sounds are also often described with onomatopoeia, as in *honk* or *beep-beep* for the horn of an automobile, and *vroom* or *brum* for the engine. For animal sounds, words like *quack* (duck), *bark* (dog), and *meow* (cat) are typically used in English.

Some other examples are: whack, fizz, crackle, hiss, whack, whir, wheeze, whine, sputter, splat, squirt, scrape, clink, clank, clunk, clatter ,crash, bang, beep, buzz, ring, rip, roar, retch, twang, toot, tinkle, thud , pop, plop, plunk, pow, snort, snuck, sniff, smack, screech, splash, squish, squeak, jingle, rattle, squeal, honk, hoot, hack, belch.

Symbol

A Symbol is a person, place, action, or thing that (by association, resemblance, or convention) represents something other than itself.

"Although symbolism works by the power of suggestion, a symbol is not the same as a meaning or a moral. A symbol cannot be an abstraction. Rather, a symbol is the thing that points to the abstraction. In short, a symbol, in general terms, is anything that stands for something else. Obvious examples are flags, which symbolize a nation; the cross is a symbol for Christianity; Uncle Sam a symbol for the United States. In Poe's 'The Raven,' death isn't the symbol; the bird is. In Crane's *The Red Badge of Courage*, courage isn't the symbol; blood is. Symbols are usually objects, but actions can also work as symbols- thus the term 'symbolic gesture.' In literature, a symbol is expected to have significance. Keats starts his ode with a real nightingale, but quickly it becomes a symbol, standing for a life of pure, unmixed joy; then before the end of the poem it becomes only a bird again.

A symbol means *more* than itself, but first it means *itself.* Like a developing image in a photographer's tray, a symbol reveals itself slowly. It's been there all along, waiting to emerge from a story, a poem or an essay. A symbol is a repeatable concrete image, an object, which captures a second level of meaning from a particular experience. A symbol is something that on the surface is its literal self but which also has another meaning or even several meanings. For example, a sword may be a sword and also symbolize justice. A symbol may be said to embody an idea. There are two general types of symbols: universal symbols that embody universally recognizable meanings wherever used, such as light to symbolize knowledge, a skull to symbolize death, etc., and constructed symbols that are given symbolic meaning by the way an author uses them in a literary work, as the white whale becomes a symbol of evil in Moby Dick.

Symbols are devices by which ideas are transmitted between people sharing a common culture. Every society has evolved a symbol system that reflects a specific cultural logic; and every symbolism functions to communicate information between members of the culture in much the same way as, but more subtly than, conventional language. Symbols tend to appear in clusters and to depend on one another for their accretion of meaning and value. They evoke a range of additional meanings beyond which are usually more abstract than its literal significance. Symbols are educational devices for evoking complex ideas without having to resort to painstaking explanations that would make a story more like an essay than an experience. Conventional symbols have meanings that are widely recognized by a society or culture. Some conventional symbols are the Christian cross, the Star of David, a swastika, or a nation's flag. Writers use conventional symbols to reinforce meanings. Kate Chopin, for example, emphasizes the spring setting in "The Story of an Hour" as a way of suggesting the renewed sense of life that Mrs. Mallard feels when she thinks herself free from her husband. A literary or contextual symbol can be a setting, character, action, object, name, or anything else in a work that maintains its literal significance while suggesting other meanings. Such symbols go beyond conventional symbols; they gain their symbolic meaning within the context of a specific story. For example, the white whale in Melville's *Moby-Dick* takes on multiple symbolic meanings in the work, but these meanings do not automatically carry over into other stories about whales. The meanings suggested by Melville's whale are specific to that text; therefore, it becomes a contextual symbol. In literature, symbols can be cultural, contextual, or personal. An object, a setting, or even a character can represent another more general idea. Allegories are narratives read in such a way that nearly every element serves as an interrelated symbol, and the narrative's meaning can be read either literally or as a symbolic statement about a political, spiritual, or psychological truth.

Imagery

Most figures of speech cast up a picture in your mind. These pictures created or suggested by the poet are called 'images'. To participate fully in the world of poem, we must understand how the poet uses image to convey more than what is actually said or literally meant.

We speak of the pictures evoked in a poem as 'imagery'. Imagery refers to the "pictures" which we perceive with our mind's eyes, ears, nose, tongue, skin, and through which we experience the "duplicate world" created by poetic language. Imagery evokes the meaning and truth of human experiences not in abstract terms, as in philosophy, but in more perceptible and tangible forms. This is a device by which the poet makes his meaning strong, clear and sure. The poet uses sound words and words of color and touch in addition to figures of speech. As well, concrete details that appeal to the reader's senses are used to build up images. Although most of the image-making words in any language appeal to sight (visual images), there are also images of touch, sound, taste, and smell.

A good poet does not use imagery merely to decorate a poem. He does not ask Himself, "How can I dress up my subject so that it will seem fancier than it is?" Rather, he asks himself, "How can I make my subject appear to the reader exactly as it appears to me?" Imagery helps him solve his problem, for it enables him to present his subject as it is: as it looks, smells, tastes, feels and sounds. To the reader imagery is equally important: it provides his imagination with something palpable to seize upon.

In this sense, imagery refers to various types of metaphors used in poetry. Even Metonymy and Synecdoche are types of metaphorical expression because they contain imagery.

Sir Philip Sidney said: "Imaging is itself the very height and life of poetry." Even before Sidney, Aristotle had stated the truth when he said, "A poet is a master of metaphor." Though he used the word 'metaphor,' what he meant was 'imagery' in general.

Conceit

Conceit is an elaborate, usually intellectually ingenious poetic comparison or image, such as an analogy or metaphor in which, say a beloved is compared to a ship, planet, etc. The comparison may be brief or extended. Read John Donne's "Valediction: Forbidding Mourning," for example, lines 21-32, where he compares his and his love's souls first to gold (which can be hammered to such a thinness that a small lump can cover the dome of a building) and then to a drawing compass whose foot in the center allows the other to draw a perfect circle:

> Our two souls therefore, which are one,
>   Though I must go, endure not yet
> A breach, but an expansion,
>   Like gold to airy thinness beat,
> If they be two, they are two so
>   As stiff twin compasses are two ;
> Thy soul, the fix'd foot, makes no show
>   To move, but doth, if the other do.
>
> And though it in the centre sit,
>   Yet, when the other far doth roam,

It leans, and hearkens after it,
And grows erect, as that comes home.

Thus a conceit is an elaborate or unusual comparison-especially one using unlikely metaphors, simile, hyperbole, and contradiction. Before the beginning of the seventeenth century, the term *conceit* was a synonym for "thought" and roughly equivalent to "idea" or "concept." It gradually came to denote a fanciful idea or a particularly clever remark. In literary terms, the word denotes a fairly elaborate figure of speech, especially an extended comparison involving unlikely metaphors, similes, imagery, hyperbole, and oxymoron.. Shakespeare also uses conceits regularly in his poetry. In *Richard II*, Shakespeare compares two kings competing for power to two buckets in a well, for instance. A conceit is usually classified as a subtype of metaphor

(4) Wit and Humour

Wit and Humour are qualities that have the potential to raise laughter. The two are attitudes to life. Wit and humour both generate laughter, but laughter from wit is a little hollow. A person is glad not to be the butt of the wit. You always laugh hardest when the wit is directed at somebody else. It is important when you are writing, because it is a great part of your characterization. Wit has a sharp edge, while humour has a tone of affection. You should be very careful when you write to keep your characters either witty or humorous, but not both. You can't have both types of people in one character. If a character is humorous, the reader is going to like him and detest the character who is witty. Of the two, humor is the more comfortable and more livable quality. Humorous persons, if their gift is genuine and not a mere shine upon the surface, are always agreeable companions and they sit through the evening best. A humorous man radiates a general pleasure and is like another candle in the room.

Humour and wit are nearly polar opposites. Humour is the tendency of particular cognitive experiences to provoke laughter and provide amusement. Humour is inclusive: it invites everyone to join in on the laugh and feel like one of the crowd. Wit is exclusive: it addresses itself only to those who are in the know. Humour is "the recognition and expression of incongruities or peculiarities in a situation or character...It illustrates some fundamental absurdity in human nature or conduct." Humor often involves someone or something being observed, there's frequently a visual or nonverbal component, and it is silly or playful. Humour is a person's disposition or temperament. It also refers to a mood; state of mind, the quality that makes something seem funny and amusing.

Wit, in contrast, is the quick apprehension and ingenuous and apt expression of the connections or analagous properties between things seemingly unlike. Wit is the sudden marriage of ideas which before their union were not perceived to have any relation. Wit, more than humour, originates in the observer; wit is highly verbal, clever and artful. "saying funny things (wit) and saying things in a funny way" (nonverbal humor). Wit, also, has more of a cutting quality than humour. Let us refer to a comparison. Letting the air out of a balloon depicts humor. Pricking an inflated balloon is wit. As Shakespeare noted, "Brevity is the soul of wit." Wit is a form of intellectual humour. A wit (referring to a person) is someone skilled in making witty remarks. Forms of wit include: the quip and the repartee. In seventeenth-century usage, the term *wit was used* much more broadly denoting originality, ingenuity, and mental acuity- especially in the sense of using paradoxes, making clever verbal expressions, and coining concise or deft phrases. As Alexander Pope put it, "True Wit is Nature to advantage dress'd, / What oft was thought, but ne'er so well express'd."

(5) Irony, Sarcasm, Satire and Paradox

Just as there are figures of speech based on comparisons between dissimilar objects or ideas, like simile and metaphor, there are figures of speech based on contrast or contradiction. Irony and paradox are the famous examples of this type.

A. Irony is a mode of expression, through words (verbal irony) or events (irony of situation), conveying a reality different from and usually opposite to appearance or expectation. A writer may say the opposite of what he means, create a reversal between expectation and its fulfillment, or give the audience knowledge that a character lacks, making the character's words have meaning to the audience not perceived by the character. In verbal irony, the writer's meaning or even his attitude may be different from what he says: "Why, no one would dare argue that there could be anything more important in choosing a college than its proximity to the beach." An example of situational irony would occur if a professional pickpocket had his own pocket picked just as he was in the act of picking someone else's pocket. The irony is generated by the surprise recognition by the audience of a reality in contrast with expectation or appearance, while another audience, victim, or character puts confidence in the appearance as reality (in this case, the pickpocket doesn't expect his own pocket to be picked). The surprise recognition by the audience often produces a comic effect, making irony often funny.

Irony takes many forms. In irony of situation, the result of an action is the reverse of what the actor expected. Macbeth murders his king hoping that in becoming king he will achieve great happiness. Actually, Macbeth never knows another moment of peace, and finally is beheaded for his murderous act. In *dramatic* irony, the audience knows something that the characters in the drama do not. For example, the identity of the murderer in a crime thriller may be known to the audience long before the mystery is solved. In *verbal* irony, the contrast is between the literal meaning of what is said and what is meant. A character may refer to a plan as "brilliant," while actually meaning that he thinks the plan is foolish.

An example of dramatic irony (where the audience has knowledge that gives additional meaning to a character's words) would be when King Oedipus, who has unknowingly killed his father, says that he will banish his father's killer when he finds him.

Irony is the most common and most efficient technique of the satirist, because it is an instrument of truth, provides wit and humor, and is usually at least obliquely critical, in that it deflates, scorns, or attacks.

The ability to detect irony is sometimes heralded as a test of intelligence and sophistication. When a text intended to be ironic is not seen as such, the effect can be disastrous. Some students have taken Swift's "Modest Proposal" literally. And Defoe's contemporaries took his "Shortest Way with the Dissenters" literally and jailed him for it. To be an effective piece of sustained irony, there must be some sort of audience tip-off, through style, tone, use of clear exaggeration, or other device. Irony: the discrepancy between what is said and what is meant, what is said and what is done, what is expected or intended and what happens, what is meant or said and what others understand. Sometimes irony is classified into types: in situational irony, expectations aroused by a situation are reversed; in <u>cosmic irony or the irony of fate,</u> misfortune is the result of fate, chance, or God; in <u>dramatic irony,</u> the audience knows more than the characters in the play, so that words and action have additional meaning for the audience; Socractic irony is named after Socrates' teaching method, whereby he assumes ignorance and openness to opposing points of view which turn out to be (he shows them to be) foolish.

In poetry, we find Verbal irony. It is a figure of speech when an expression used is the opposite of the thought in the speaker's mind, thus conveying a meaning that contradicts the literal definition. <u>Dramatic irony</u> is a literary or theatrical device of having a character utter words which the reader or audience understands to have a different meaning, but of which the character himself is unaware. <u>Irony of situation</u> is when a situation occurs which is quite the reverse of what one might have expected. Often, Frost's use of irony conveys one meaning by word and syntax, and another by the tone of voice it indicates. The tone contradicts the words. Frost's irony is usually tricky because it is so subtle. Look at the following examples from Robert Frost's poetry: In *Birches,* the wish to get away from earth may not be granted too soon leads to Dramatic irony. In *Range-Finding,* Irony of situation arises when the spider is disturbed by a bullet but finds it unimportant. The poem *The Road Not Taken* offers an example of Verbal irony: the speaker knows he will tell the old story "with a sigh" of a choice that "made all the difference."

Irony is often confused with sarcasm and satire :

Sarcasm is one kind of irony; it is praise which is really an insult; sarcasm generally involves malice, the desire to put someone down, e.g., "This is my brilliant son, who failed out of college." Satire is the exposure of the vices or follies of an individual or a group, an institution, an idea, a society, etc., usually with a view to correcting it. Satirists frequently use irony. Irony does not necessarily have to do with retribution as people have been stating. Irony is when the opposite of what you expect occurs, or when someone says something to mean the opposite of its literal meaning. For example, if Joe says he got in a car accident and you reply "What a happy day," you would be being ironic, because of course you're pointing out that the day was anything BUT happy.

B. Satire is a literary mode based on criticism of people and society through ridicule. The satirist aims to reduce the practices attacked by laughing scornfully at them- and being witty enough to allow the reader to laugh, also. Ridicule, irony, exaggeration, and several other techniques are almost always present. The satirist may insert serious statements of value or desired behavior, but most often he relies on an implicit moral code, understood by his audience and paid lip service by them. The satirist's goal is to point out the hypocrisy of his target in the hope that either the target or the audience will return to a real following of the code. Thus, satire is inescapably moral even when no explicit values are promoted in the work, for the satirist works within the framework of a widely spread value system. Many of the techniques of satire are devices of comparison, to show the similarity or contrast between two things.

Satire is a piece of literature designed to ridicule the subject of the work. While satire can be funny, its aim is not to amuse, but to arouse contempt, and hopefully to "correct" vice or folly. Jonathan swift's *Gulliver's Travels* satirizes the English people, making them seem dwarfish in their ability to deal with large thoughts, issues, or deeds. Satire arouses laughter or scorn as a means of ridicule and derision, with the avowed intention of correcting human faults. Common targets of satire include individuals (*personal* satire), types of people, social groups, institutions, and human nature. Like tragedy and comedy, satire is often a mode of writing introduced into various literary forms; it is only a genre when it is the governing principle of a work. In *direct* satire, a first-person speaker addresses either the reader or a character within the work whose conversation helps further the speaker's purposes, as in Alexander Pope's *Epistle to Dr. Arbuthnot* (1735). *Indirect* satire uses a fictional narrative in which characters who represent particular points of view are made ridiculous by their own behaviour and thoughts, and by the narrator's usually ironic commentary. In Jonathan Swift's *Gulliver's Travels* (1726) the hero narrating his own adventures appears ridiculous in taking pride in his Lilliputian title of honour, "Nardac"; by making Gulliver look foolish in this way, Swift indirectly satirizes the pretensions of the English nobility, with its corresponding titles of "Duke" and "Marquess."

Juvenalian Satire refers to harsher, more pointed, perhaps intolerant satire typified by the writings of Juvenal. Juvenalian satire often attacks particular people, sometimes thinly disguised as fictional characters. While laughter and ridicule are still weapons as with Horatian satire, the Juvenalian satirist also uses withering invective and a slashing attack. Jonathan Swift and Alexander Pope are Juvenalian satirists.

C. Sarcasm is a form of sneering criticism in which disapproval is often expressed as ironic praise. (Oddly enough, sarcastic remarks are often used between friends, perhaps as a somewhat perverse demonstration of the strength of the bond-only a good friend could say this without hurting the other's feelings, or at least without excessively damaging the relationship, since feelings are often hurt in spite of a close relationship. If you drop your lunch tray and a stranger says, "Well, that was really intelligent," that's sarcasm. If your girlfriend or boyfriend says it, that's love- I think.) Sarcasm is a form of verbal irony.

Sarcasm is a sharp, bitter, or cutting expression or remark; a bitter jibe or taunt. Some authorities sharply distinguish sarcasm from irony, however others argue that sarcasm may or often does involve irony. In sarcasm, ridicule or mockery is used harshly, often crudely and contemptuously, for destructive purposes. It may be used in an indirect manner, and have the form of irony, as in "What a fine musician you turned out to be!" or it may be used in the form of a direct statement, "You couldn't play one piece correctly if you had two assistants." The distinctive quality of sarcasm is present in the spoken word and manifested chiefly by voice quality.

D. Paradox is a statement that initially appears to be contradictory but then, on closer inspection, turns out to make sense. It refers to a situation or a statement that seems to contradict itself, but on closer inspection, does not. For example, John Donne ends his sonnet "Death, Be Not Proud" with the paradoxical statement "Death, thou shalt die." Also look at thee lines from Donne's another poem, *Holy Sonnet 10: T*hat I may rise, and stand, overthrow me. The poet paradoxically asks God to knock him down so that he may stand. What he means by this is for God to destroy his present self and remake him as a holier person. To solve the paradox, it is necessary to discover the sense that underlies the statement. Paradox is useful in poetry because it arrests a reader's attention by its seemingly stubborn refusal to make sense.

Paradox thus is a statement or situation containing apparently contradictory or incompatible elements, but on closer inspection may be true. According to New Critics, the use of paradox , along with that of irony, has been considered strength of great poetry.

Cleanth Brooks has analysed the use of these two figures of speech in Donne's poetry. Wordsworth's line "Child is father of the Man" is a famous example. Look at Frost's line from his poem, *The Tuft of Flowers*: "Men work together whether they work together or apart."

(6) Genre

Genre, is a French term for a type, species, or class of composition. A literary genre is a recognizable and established category of written work employing common conventions so that it will prevent readers or audiences from mistaking it for another kind. Genre, in literature, refers to a class or type of literary work, such as epic, lyric, tragedy, or comedy. In classical literature the genres were carefully distinguished from each other not only by subject-matter but also by formal aspects such as dialect, vocabulary, and metre, and the conventions of each genre were strictly adhered to. Ignorance of these has sometimes resulted in misplaced criticism, as when Samuel Johnson found 'inherently improbable' the pastoral elegy *Lycidas* by *the poet Milton*..

Much of the confusion surrounding the term 'Genre' arises from the fact that it is used simultaneously for the most basic modes of literary art (lyric, narrative, dramatic); for the broadest categories of composition (poetry, prose fiction), and for more specialized sub-categories, which are defined according to several different criteria including formal structure (sonnet, picaresque novel), length (novella, epigram), intention (satire), effect (comedy), origin (folktale), and subject matter (pastoral, science fiction). While some genres, such as the pastoral elegy or the melodrama, have numerous conventions governing subject, style, and form, others have no agreed rules, although they may include several more limited subgenres.

Generally, the three broadest categories of *genre* include poetry, drama, and fiction. These general *genres* are often subdivided into more specific *genres* and *subgenres*. For instance, precise examples of *genres* might include murder mysteries, westerns, sonnets, lyric poetry, epics and tragedies. Many bookstores and video stores divide their books or films into *genres* for the convenience of shoppers seeking a specific category of literature.

When we say a poem, novel, story, or other literary work belongs to a particular genre, it shares at least a few conventions, or standard characteristics, with other works in that genre. For example, works in the Gothic genre often feature supernatural elements, attempts to horrify the reader, and dark, foreboding settings, particularly very old castles or mansions. Edgar Allan Poe's short story "The Fall of the House of Usher" belongs to the Gothic genre because it takes place in a gloomy mansion that seems to exert supernatural control over a man who lives in it. Furthermore, Poe attempts to horrify the reader by describing the man's ghastly face, the burial of his sister, eerie sounds in the house, and ultimately the reappearance of the sister's bloody body at the end of the story. Other genres include the pastoral poem, epic poem, elegy, and tragic drama. An understanding of genre is useful because it helps us to see how an author adopts or transcends the standard practices that other authors have developed.

(7) Interior Monologue and Stream of Consciousness
Stream of Consciousness

In literary criticism, stream of consciousness is a narrative mode that seeks to portray an individual's point of view by giving the written equivalent of the character's thought processes, either in a loose interior monologue, or in connection to his or her actions. Writers who create stream-of-consciousness works of literature focus on the emotional and psychological processes that are taking place in the minds of one or more characters. Important character traits are revealed through an exploration of what is going on in the mind.

Stream-of-consciousness writing is usually regarded as a special form of interior monologue and is characterized by associative leaps in syntax and punctuation that can make the prose difficult to follow. Stream of consciousness and interior monologue are distinguished from dramatic monologue, where the speaker is addressing an audience or a third person, and is used chiefly in poetry or drama. In stream of consciousness, the speaker's thought processes are more often depicted as overheard in the mind (or addressed to oneself); it is primarily a fictional device. The term was introduced to the field of literary studies from that of psychology, where it was coined by philosopher and psychologist William James in 1890. It is a literary technique which was pioneered by Dorothy Richardson, Virginia Woolf, and James Joyce. It is characterized by a flow of thoughts and images, which may not always appear to have a coherent structure or cohesion. The plot line may weave in and out of time and place, carrying the reader through the life span of a character or further along a timeline to incorporate the lives (and thoughts) of characters from other time periods.

Stream of consciousness is either the continuous flow of sense perceptions, thoughts, feelings, and memories in the human mind or is a literary method of representing such a blending of mental processes in fictional characters, usually in an unpunctuated or disjointed form of interior monologue. The term is often used as a synonym for interior monologue, but they can also be distinguished, in two ways. In the first (psychological) sense, the stream of consciousness is the subject matter while interior monologue is the technique for presenting it; thus Marcel Proust's novel *A la recherche du temps perdu* (1913–27) is *about* the stream of consciousness, especially the connection between sense impressions and memory, but it does not actually use interior monologue. In the second (literary) sense, stream of consciousness is a special style of interior monologue: while an interior monologue always presents a character's thoughts 'directly', without the apparent intervention of a summarizing and selecting narrator, it does not necessarily mingle them with impressions and perceptions, nor does it necessarily violate the norms of grammar, syntax, and logic; but the stream of consciousness technique also does one or both of these things. An important device of modernist fiction and its later imitators, the technique was pioneered by Dorothy Richardson in *Pilgrimage* (1915–35) and by James Joyce in *Ulysses* (1922), and further developed by Virginia Woolf in *Mrs Dalloway* (1925), *The Waves* (1931) and William Faulkner in *The Sound and the Fury* (1928).

Stream of consciousness, in literature, is a technique that records the multifarious thoughts and feelings of a character without regard to logical argument or narrative sequence. The writer attempts by the stream of consciousness to reflect all the forces, external and internal, influencing the psychology of a character at a single moment.

Interior Monologue

Primarily associated with the modernist movement, stream of consciousness is a form of interior monologue which claims as its goal the representation of a lead consciousness in a narrative (typically fiction). This representation of consciousness can include perceptions or impressions, thoughts incited by outside sensory stimuli, and fragments of random, disconnected thoughts. Stream of consciousness writing often lacks "correct" punctuation or syntax, favoring a looser, more incomplete style.

Gerald Prince contests the term's frequent association with "interior monologue in his *Dictionary of Narratology,* writing:

Though interior monologue and stream of consciousness have often been considered interchangeable, they have also frequently been contrasted: the former would present a character's thoughts rather than impressions or perceptions, while the latter would present both impressions and thoughts; or else, the former would respect morphology and syntax, whereas the latter would not...and would thus capture thought in its nascent stage, prior to any logical connection.

Interior monologue is a tool through which a writer can exhibit the thoughts of the characters to the readers. Shakespeare used interior monologue in the form of a soliloquy (where a character speaks to himself, thus revealing his thoughts). Many fiction writers use interior monologue to show the mental state of a character, his doubts, fears, plans, secrets or anything that he may be feeling or thinking about.

Direct interior monologue

As its name suggests, direct interior monologue is directly spoken by a character without any authorial intervention. It is a part of the dialogue and is within inverted commas. A character can reveal his thoughts to the reader by directly reacting to a situation. It affords the writer greater freedom. *"I hate going to Myna's Palace," he thought, dragging his legs forward.* This dialogue demonstrates the contradiction between how a character acts and what is going on in his mind. He doesn't want to go, but he still is.

In direct interior monologue, there is no chance of intervention by the author. It is the character who is in focus, not the author. An advantage of direct interior monologue is that through it, a writer can show instant happenings as well as reminiscences. A character may pass on judgments about other characters, he may comment upon the situation, scenery, characteristics and so on.

Indirect interior monologue

When the author comments upon the thoughts of a character, it is called indirect interior monologue. Stream of consciousness is a form of free interior monologue where a character's thoughts are presented as random as they occur in his mind. It should be used only when required. Here is an example of stream of consciousness from James Joyce's *Ulysses*. It presents the thoughts of Molly Bloom.

. . . yes because they're so weak and puling when they're sick they want a woman to get well if his nose bleeds you'd think it was so tragic and that dying looking one off the south circular when he sprained his foot at the choir party at the sugarloaf Mountain the day I wore that dress Miss Stack bringing him flowers the worst old ones she could find at the bottom of the basket anything at all to get into a mans bedroom with her old maids voice . . .

Indirect interior monologue becomes exciting when the author's voice creeps in just a bit to add a feeling to a sentence. It goes like this -

*You dipped it in!" Mira exclaimed, looking at the swollen pancake floating in the water with utter astonishment. **Such megalomania could only be expected from Mira.***

The sentence in bold is an indirect monologue, as the opinion about Mira is being hinted by the author (and quite boldly), not by any of the characters. The reader might not have judged till now that Mira has a huge ego, but when the writer so forcefully dictates it in a sentence, the reader, at once, starts to see her in that light.

The biggest advantage of indirect interior monologue is that it surprises the readers and shakes them out of the lull that narration causes. It works best when used while giving a forceful or a sharp opinion about somebody or something. As it is part of the narration and not of a dialogue, it creates a strong impression on the reader's mind, as the opinion is of the author and not a character. That is why it becomes much more believable. Sprinkling indirect interior monologue in writing is a good method to surprise and instruct the reader at the same time.

A drawback with indirect interior monologue is that the author can't relate instant happenings or describe action. He has to rely upon general thoughts or opinions about characters or their situation.

Difference

Stream-of-consciousness narration is a variant of the limited third-person point of vew; the narrator relates only what is experienced by a character's mind from moment to moment, presenting life as thought process, or interior monologue. Mcre precisely, "stream of consciousness" refers to any lengthy passages of introspection in literature; whereas "interior monologue" denotes a narrative entirely in a wandering, introspective style. James Joyce's *Ulysses* (1922) experiments in types of stream-of-consciousness narrative, while Virginia Woolf's *Mrs. Dalloway* (1925) is an example of a series of interior monologues:

It seemed to her as she drank the sweet stuff that she was opening long windows, stepping out into some garden. But where? The clock was striking- one, two, three: how sensible the sound was; compared with all this thumping; like Septimus himself. She was falling asleep.

Interior Monologue is a narrative technique in fiction intended to render the flow of myriad impressions - visual, auditory, tactile, associative, and subliminal - that impinge on an individual consciousness. To represent the mind at work, a writer may incorporate snatches of thought and grammatical constructions that do not seem coherent because they are based on the free association of ideas and images. In the 20th century, writers attempting to capture the total flow of their characters' consciousness commonly used the techniques of interior monologue, which represents a sequence of thought and feeling.

Interior monologue is the direct presentation of thought as in direct speech. One does not speak of a monologue unless the utterance has a certain length. Interior monologue is thus a longish passage of uninterrupted thought. Obviously, interior monologue is a technique that puts a certain amount of strain on the reader. Thus, it is more common to learn about a character's consciousness from the narrator, who takes it upon him- or herself, to report the character's thoughts to the reader.

Interior monologue is one particular kind of *stream of consciousness* writing. Stream of consciousness writing aims to provide a textual equivalent to the imagined stream of consciousness in the mind of a fictional character. Writers wanted to display for readers' inspection, in a way that is impossible in real life, their characters' private inner lives. These were imagined as containing many different kinds of "mind stuff," as it was called by William James: verbalised thoughts, subliminal thoughts, perceptions, images and sensations.

(8) Setting

In fiction, setting includes the time, location, and everything in which a story takes place, and initiates the main backdrop and mood for a story. When and where a story takes place is called the setting. It has been referred to as story world or milieu to include a context (especially society) beyond the immediate surroundings of the story. Elements of setting may include culture, historical period, and geography. Along with plot, character, theme, and style, setting is considered one of the fundamental components of fiction. A setting is the time, place and social environment a story takes place.

Setting is a key role in plot, as in man vs. nature or man vs. society stories. In some stories the setting becomes a character itself. In such roles setting may be considered a plot structure or literary device. The term "setting" is often used to refer to the social milieu in which the events of a novel occur.

The setting may be nothing more than the backdrop for what occurs; however, it may be directly linked to mood or meaning. It can create an atmosphere that affects our response to the work. It may have a direct effect on a character's motivation. An external force may enter the setting and change it, causing conflict for the characters. The physical details of the setting are linked with the values, ideals, and attitudes of a place in different times. Setting can add an important dimension of meaning, reflecting character and embodying theme.

A critic says, "Every story would be another story, and unrecognizable if it took up its characters and plot and happened somewhere else... Fiction depends for its life on place. Place is the crossroads of circumstance, the proving ground of what happens and to whom."

Writers describe the world they know. Sights, sounds, colors, and textures are all vividly painted in words as an artist paints images on canvas. A writer imagines a story to be happening in a place that is rooted in his or her mind. The location of a story's actions, along with the time in which it occurs, is the setting. Considering which aspects of setting are significant in determining the fate of the protagonist is frequently a clue to the underlying meaning of a story. If the time or place setting of the story changes, we should consider how those changes alter the outcome of the story.

Setting is created by language. How many or how few details we learn is up to the author. Many authors leave a lot of these details up to the reader's imagination. At times the setting can be real, though the details are imaginary. The setting of Thomas Hardy's Wessex novels or the setting of Malgudi in R.K. Narayan's novels are the famous examples

(9) Classicism, Neo-Classicism, Romanticism, Realism, Naturalism, the Absurd, Modernism, Symbolism

1. Classicism

Classicism refers to an attitude to literature that is guided by admiration of the qualities of formal balance, proportion, decorum, and restraint attributed to the major works of ancient Greek and Roman literature ('the classics') in preference to the irregularities of later vernacular literatures, and especially (since about 1800) to the artistic liberties proclaimed by Romanticism. A *classic* is a work of the highest class, and it generally follows in the footsteps of classicism.. During and since the Renaissance, these overlapping meanings came to be applied to the writings of major Greek and Roman authors from Homer to Juvenal, which were regarded as unsurpassed models of excellence. The adjective *classical,* usually applied to this body of writings, has since been extended to outstandingly creative periods of other literatures: the 17th century may be regarded as the classical age of French literature. A classical style or approach to literary composition is usually one that imitates Greek or Roman models in subject matter or in form by the adoption of forms like tragedy, epic, ode, or verse satire, or both. As a literary doctrine, classicism holds that the writer must be governed by rules, models, or conventions, rather than by wayward inspiration: in its most strictly codified form in the 17th and 18th centuries, by what was called Neoclassicism. It required the observance of rules derived from Aristotle's *Poetics* and Horace's *Ars Poetica,* principally those of decorum and the dramatic unities.. After the end of the 18th century, 'classical' came to be contrasted with 'romantic' in an opposition of increasingly generalized terms embracing moods and attitudes as well as characteristics of actual works. Since then, literary classicism has often been less a matter of imitating Greek and Roman models than of resisting the claims of Romanticism and all that it may be thought to stand for, namely Protestantism, liberalism, democracy, anarchy. The critical doctrines of Matthew Arnold, and more especially of T. S. Eliot, are classicist in this sense of reacting against the Romantic principle of unrestrained self expression.

Classicism, applied generally, means clearness, elegance, symmetry, and repose produced by attention to traditional forms. Because the principles of classicism were derived from the rules and practices of the ancients, the term came to mean the adherence to specific academic canons. They are as follows:

1. Imitation of antiquity: The theorists of classicism saw literature as working in a tradition which went back to the great writers of antiquity.

2. Truth to nature: It means finding the best possible way of writing about *human* nature, seen not so much in its local manifestations as in its unchanging essence.

3. Reason: Closely associated with truth to nature, reason does, however, imply a taste for order, measure, and harmony. In its social manifestation it enjoins the writer to observe decorum.

d. Instruction and Pleasure: All critics spoke of the didactic function of poetry. But while writers had a duty to instruct, they were no less obliged to give pleasure which, indeed, makes instruction possible.

2. Neoclassicism

The term "Neoclassicism" (derived from "neo", Greek for new, or revived, and "classicism", referring to the work of Greek and Latin authors) summarises an aesthetic that draws on ancient models for its guide and inspiration. In English literature it is a term particularly used to describe the writings of the later-seventeenth to the late eighteenth centuries, a period that includes the major achievements of John Dryden (1631-1700) at one end, of Alexander Pope (1688-1744) in the middle and of Samuel Johnson (1709-84) at the other.

To a certain extent Neoclassicism represented a reaction against the optimistic, exuberant, and enthusiastic Renaissance view of man as a being fundamentally good and possessed of an infinite potential for spiritual and intellectual growth. Neoclassical theorists, by contrast, saw man as an imperfect being, inherently sinful, whose potential was limited. They replaced the Renaissance emphasis on the imagination, on invention and experimentation, and on mysticism with an emphasis on order and reason, on restraint, on common sense, and on religious, political, economic and philosophical conservatism. They maintained that man himself was the most appropriate subject of art, and saw art itself as essentially pragmatic and as something which was properly intellectual rather than emotional. Hence their emphasis on proper subject matter and on concepts like symmetry, proportion, unity, harmony, and grace, which would facilitate the process of delighting, instructing, educating, and correcting the social animal which they believed man to be.

Always aware of the conventions appropriate to each genre, Neoclassicists modeled their works on classical masterpieces and heeded the "rules" thought to be laid down by classical critics. In political and social affairs, too, they were guided by the wisdom of the past: traditional institutions had, at least, survived the test of time. No more than their medieval and Renaissance predecessors did neoclassical thinkers share our modern assumption that change means progress, since they believed that human nature is imperfect, human achievements are necessarily limited, and therefore human aims should be sensibly limited as well. It was better to set a moderate goal, whether in art or society, and achieve it well, than to strive for an infinite ideal and fail.

Neoclassical thinkers assumed that human nature was constant. Art should express this essential nature: "Nothing can please many, and please long, but just representations of general nature," said Samuel Johnson. An individual character was valuable for what he or she revealed of universal human nature. Neoclassical artists did not strive to be original so much as to express old truths in a newly effective way. As Alexander Pope, one of their greatest poets, wrote: "True wit is nature to advantage dressed, / What oft was thought, but ne'er so well expressed." Neoclassical writers aimed to articulate general truth rather than unique vision, to communicate to others more than to express themselves.

Neoclassicism was a movement whose artists looked to the classical texts for their creative inspiration in an effort to imitate classical form. The writers in particular drew on what were considered to be classical virtues- simplicity, order, restraint, logic, economy, accuracy, and decorum- to produce prose, poetry, and drama. Literature was of value in accordance with its ability to not only delight, but also instruct.

Although the terms Classicism and Neoclassicism are somewhat interchangeable, Neoclassicism refers strictly the specific literary periods in history that produced art inspired by the ancients, which, of course, excludes the ancients themselves. It is usually more specifically defined as a Classicism that originally dominated English literature during the Restoration Age and which lasted well into the eighteenth century.

3. Romanticism

It is one of the curiosities of literary history that the strongholds of the Romantic Movement were England and Germany, not the countries of the romance languages themselves. Thus it is from the historians of English and German literature that we inherit the convenient set of terminal dates for the Romantic period, beginning in 1798, the year of the first edition of *Lyrical Ballads* by Wordsworth and Coleridge.

Romantic poets cultivated individualism, reverence for the natural world, idealism, physical and emotional passion, and an interest in the mystic and supernatural. Romantics set themselves in opposition to the order and rationality of classical and neoclassical artistic precepts to embrace freedom and revolution in their art and politics. German romantic poets included Fredrich Schiller and Johann Wolfgang von Goethe, and British poets such as William Wordsworth, Samuel Taylor Coleridge, Percy Bysshe Shelley, George Gordon Lord Byron, and John Keats propelled the English Romantic movement. Victor Hugo was a noted French Romantic poet as well, and romanticism crossed the Atlantic through the work of American poets like Walt Whitman and Edgar Allan Poe. The Romantic era produced many of the stereotypes of poets and poetry that exist to this day (i.e., the poet as a highly tortured and melancholy visionary).

"Nature" meant many things to the Romantics. As suggested above, it was often presented as itself a work of art, constructed by a divine imagination, in emblematic language. Romantic nature poetry is essentially a poetry of meditation. Symbolism and myth were given great prominence in the Romantic conception of art. In the Romantic view, symbols were the human aesthetic correlatives of nature's emblematic language. They were valued too because they could simultaneously suggest many things, and were thus thought superior to the one-to-one communications of allegory. Partly, it may have been the desire to express the "inexpressible"- the infinite- through the available resources of language that led to symbol at one level and myth as symbolic narrative) at another. Emphasis on the activity of the imagination was accompanied by greater emphasis on the importance of intuition, instincts, and feelings, and Romantics generally called for greater attention to the emotions as a necessary supplement to purely logical reason. When this emphasis was applied to the creation of poetry, a very important shift of focus occurred. Wordsworth's definition of all good poetry as "the spontaneous overflow of powerful feelings" marks a turning point in literary history. By locating the ultimate source of poetry in the individual artist, the tradition, stretching back to the ancients, of valuing art primarily for its ability to imitate human life (that is, for its mimetic qualities) was reversed. In Romantic theory, art was valuable not so much as a mirror of the external world, but as a source of illumination of the world within.

4. Realism

Literary realism most often refers to the trend, beginning with certain works of 19th century French literature and extending to late-nineteenth- and early-twentieth-century authors in various countries, towards depictions of contemporary life and society "as they were." In the spirit of general "realism," Realist authors opted for depictions of everyday and banal activities and experiences, instead of a romanticized or similarly stylized presentation.

George Eliot's novel *Middlemarch* stands as a great milestone in the realist tradition. It is a primary example of nineteenth-century realism's role in the naturalization of the burgeoning capitalist marketplace.

William Dean Howells was the first American author to bring a realist aesthetic to the literature of the United States. Balzac is often credited with pioneering a systematic realism in French literature, through the inclusion of specific detail and recurring characters. Flaubert is regarded by many critics as representing the zenith of the realist style with his unadorned prose and attention to the details of everyday life. Later "realist" writers included Emile Zola, whose naturalism is often regarded as an offshoot of realism.

Realism in literature refers to the general attempt to depict subjects "in accordance with secular empirical rules," as they are considered to exist in third person objective reality, without embellishment or interpretation. As Ian Watt states, modern realism "begins from the position that truth can be discovered by the individual through the senses" and as such "it has its origins in Decartes and Locke.

Realism often refers more specifically to the artistic movement, which began in <u>France</u> in the 1850s. Realism believed in the ideology of objective reality and revolted against the exaggerated emotionalism of the romantic movement. Truth and accuracy became the goals of many Realists. Many paintings which sprung up during the time of realism depicted people at work, as during the 19th century there were many open work places due to the Industrial and Commercial Revolutions. The popularity of such 'realistic' works grew with the introduction of photography - a new visual source that created a desire for people to produce representations which look "objectively real."

Realist writers sought to narrate their novels from an objective, unbiased perspective that simply and clearly represented the factual elements of the story. They became masters at psychological characterization, detailed descriptions of everyday life in realistic settings, and dialogue that captures the idioms of natural human speech. The realists endeavored to accurately represent contemporary culture and people from all walks of life. Thus, realist writers often addressed themes of socioeconomic conflict by contrasting the living conditions of the poor with those of the upper classes in urban as well as rural societies.

Some other prominent exponents of realism are Gustave Flaubert, Guy de Maupassant, Turgenev, Dostoevsky, and Leo Tolstoy. In England, the foremost realist authors were Charles Dickens, George Eliot, and Anthony Trollope. In the United States, William Dean Howells was the foremost realist writer. Naturalism, an offshoot of Realism, was a literary movement that placed even greater emphasis on the accurate representation of details from contemporary life. In the United

States, Regionalism and local color fiction in particular were American offshoots of Realism.

5. Naturalism

Naturalism, in literature, is an approach that proceeds from an analysis of reality in terms of natural forces, e.g., heredity, environment, physical drives. The chief literary theorist on naturalism was Émile Zola, who said in 1880 that the novelist should be like the scientist, examining dispassionately various phenomena in life and drawing indisputable conclusions. The naturalists tended to concern themselves with the harsh, often sordid, aspects of life. In the drama, naturalism developed in the late 19th century. By stressing photographic detail in scene design, costume, and acting technique, it attempted to abolish the artificial theatricality prominent in 19th-century theatre.

Naturalism, a literary movement taking place from 1880s to 1940s, used detailed realism to suggest that social conditions, heredity, and environment had inescapable force in shaping human character. It sought to replicate a believable everyday reality, as opposed to such movements as Romanticism or Surrealism, in which subjects may receive highly symbolic, idealistic, or even supernatural treatment. Naturalism is the outgrowth of Realism of mid-19th-century France and elsewhere. Naturalistic writers were influenced by the evolution theory of Charles Darwin. They believed that one's heredity and social environment determine one's character. Whereas realism seeks only to describe subjects as they really are, naturalism also attempts to determine "scientifically" the underlying forces influencing the actions of its subjects. Naturalistic works often include uncouth or sordid subject matter; for example, Emile Zola's works had a frankness about sexuality along with a pervasive pessimism. Naturalistic works exposed the dark harshness of life, including poverty, racism, sex, prejudice, disease, prostitution, and filth. As a result, naturalistic writers were frequently criticized for being too blunt.

There are defining characteristics of naturalistic fiction. They are: 1. Pessimism 2. Detachment 3. Objectivity 4. Determinism 5. Surprising twist at the end of the narrative. 6. Nature is indifferent to human struggle.

In the United States, the genre is associated principally with writers such as Stephen Crane, Steinbeck, Edith Wharton and most prominently

Frank Norris, and Theodore Dreiser. Although Zola was a touchstone of contemporary debates over genre, Dreiser, perhaps the most important of the naturalist writers, regarded Balzac as a greater influence. American naturalism, as a concept, uses two direct approaches in its definition. The first is that naturalism as an outgrowth of realism and taking the same direction as realism, it simply continues realism but taking a different method. The second approach is the difference that identifies naturalism from realism. The biggest difference between realism and naturalism as agreed upon by most critics agree is the philosophical bent in the works of the naturalists. Due to this, American naturalism is being viewed as basically realism with an added gloomy determinism.

Realism vs Naturalism in Literature

Though naturalism and realism are inter-related, they are different from each other. Here are a few differences between realism and naturalism:

- The history of naturalism in literature can be traced back to the nineteenth century and naturalism was supposed to be the extreme form of realism. As compared to romanticism and realism, naturalism is a more recent movement in the literary cycle.

- The focus of realism is on literary technique, whereas naturalism connotes a philosophical pessimism, where writers apply scientific method to their writings and depict human beings as an objective and impartial character.

- Realism portrays things the way they might appear to be, while naturalism shows a deterministic view of a person's life and actions. This can be seen in Stephen Crane's *The Open Boat* and *The Blue Hotel*

Realism shows that a person's decision is based upon his response to the situation, whereas naturalism concludes that a person's decision is predetermined by natural forces that make him act in a certain way.

6. The Absurd

"The Absurd", in philosophy, refers to the clash between the human tendency to seek inherent meaning and the human inability to find any. In this context "absurd" does not mean "logically impossible," but rather "humanly impossible." The universe and the human mind do not each separately cause the Absurd, but rather, the Absurd arises by the contradictory reality caused by the confrontation of both, simultaneously.

Absurdism, therefore, is a philosophy stating that the efforts of humanity to find inherent meaning in the universe will ultimately fail (and hence are absurd), because no such meaning exists, at least in relation to the individual. As a philosophy, absurdism also explores the fundamental nature of the Absurd and how human individuals, once becoming conscious of the Absurd, should react to it.

Absurdism is very closely related to existentialism and nihilism and has its origins in the 19th century Danish philosopher, Soren Kierkegaard, who chose to confront the crisis humans faced with the Absurd by developing existential philosophy. Absurdism as a belief system was born of the European existentialist movement that ensued, specifically when the French philosopher and writer Albert Camus rejected certain aspects from that philosophical line of thought and published his manuscript *The Myth of Sisyphus (1942)*. The aftermath of World War II provided the social environment that stimulated absurdist views and allowed for their popular development, especially in the devastated country of France.

The Absurd encompasses the following:

The world is absurd. Existence *is* without reason. If there is a god, such a god is absent and either without much power or is evil to the core for allowing the kinds of nonsense that happens every day on this planet. If there is divinity, it's as if a cold, heartless mischievousness rules the universe. We are thrown into the world without a clue as to why or as to what we're to do. And where are we headed? There is no answer.

Kierkegaard believed that the absurdity of a god become human, become flesh, a god who dies on a cross - what could be more absurd? To say yes, I must have faith in such an absurd incarnation is Kierkegaard's answer. We can take the leap of faith and say yes to the absurdity of the world.

Nietzsche proclaimed the death of God, saying in some sense that the grand story which had provided meaning to our lives and our culture, has lost its power. We are adrift in meaninglessness. The absurd seeps toward us like the stench of a dead god.

Camus tells us the story of Sisyphus, the mythical figure who was eternally condemned by the gods to push a huge bolder up a hill only to watch it tumble back down each time he was about to reach the top. At that moment, Sisyphus could do nothing but start over. This is our lot in life. Nothing ever turns out exactly as we would have hoped or would have expected. Given no blueprint for living, we face huge questions that we must answer ourselves, and when the results are not as we had hoped, we must begin again. Try again. What else is there to do? Therefore Camus endorsed a solution that one should accept the Absurd and continues to live in spite of it, believing that by accepting the Absurd, one had achieved absolute freedom, by recognizing no religious or other moral contraints and that in revolting against the Absurd while simultaneously accepting it as unstoppable, one could possibly be content from the personal meaning constructed in the process.

Sartre explains the absurd nothingness of human existence. There is no human nature, no essence. We are literally no-thing, and thus are always in the process of creating ourselves, never finished, never justified, condemned to accept complete responsibility for what we do on earth, so radically free that we find ourselves in charge of creating the very values that will guide us into and through a world with others.

7. Modernism

Modernist literature is the literary expression of the tendencies of Modernism, especially High Modernism. Modernistic art and literature normally revolved around the idea of individualism, mistrust of institutions (government, religion), and the disbelief of any absolute truths. Modernism as a literary movement reached its height in Europe between 1900 and the middle 1920s. Modernist literature addressed aesthetic problems similar to those examined in non-literary forms of contemporaneous Modernist art.

"The deepest problems of modern life derive from the claim of the individual to preserve the autonomy and individuality of his existence in the face of overwhelming social forces, of historical heritage, of external culture, and of the technique of life."

The Modernist re-contextualization of the individual within the fabric of this received social heritage can be seen in the "mythic method" which T.S. Eliot expounded in his discussion of James Joyce's *Ulysses*:

"In using the myth, in manipulating a continuous parallel between contemporaneity and antiquity, Mr. Joyce is pursuing a method which others must pursue after him ... It is simply a way of controlling, of ordering, of giving a shape and a significance to the immense panorama of futility and anarchy which is contemporary history."

- ○ Modernism is marked by a strong and intentional break with tradition. This break includes a strong reaction against established religious, political, and social views.
- ○ Modernists believe the world is created in the act of perceiving it; that is, the world is what we say it is.
- ○ Modernists do not subscribe to absolute truth. All things are relative.
- ○ Modernists feel no connection with history or institutions. Their experience is that of alienation, loss, and despair.
- ○ Modernists champion the individual and celebrate inner strength.
- ○ Modernists believe life is unordered.
- ○ Modernists concern themselves with the sub-conscious.

    Modernism is marked by experimentation, particularly manipulation of form , and by the realization that knowledge is not absolute. Significant works are:

- ○ James Joyce - His most experimental and famous work, *Ulysses*, completely abandons generally accepted notions of plot, setting, and characters.
- ○ Virginia Woolf - *To the Lighthouse*, as well, strays from conventional forms, focusing on Stream of Consciousness.
- ○ D.H. Lawrence - His novels reflected on the dehumanizing effect of modern society.
- ○ T.S. Eliot - Although American, Eliot's *The Wasteland* is associated with London and emphasizes the emptiness of Industrialism.

Known as "The Lost Generation" American writers of the 1920s brought Modernism to the United States. For writers like Hemingway and Fitzgerald, World War I destroyed the illusion that acting virtuously did bring about good.

The following general features/ ideas/ attitudes are underlined in Modernism:

(1) Modernism was built on a sense of lost community and civilization and embodied a series of contradictions and paradoxes, embraced multiple features of modern sensibility. (2) Revolution and conservatism. (3) Loss of a sense of tradition. (4) Celebrated as a means of liberation from the past. (5) Aesthetics of experimentation. (6) Fragmentation (7) Ambiguity. (8) Nihilism. (9) Intentional distortion of shapes (10) Focus on form rather than meaning (11) Breakdown of social norms and cultural values. (12) Disillusionment. (13) Rejection of history and the substitution of a mythical past. (14) Importance of the unconscious mind. (15). Impossibility of an absolute interpretation of reality. (16) Ideological uncertainty. (17) Historical and material determinism.

Characteristics : Modernism in Literature:

- uses images ("word pictures") and symbols as typical and frequent literary techniques

- uses colloquial language rather than formal language

- uses language in a very self-conscious way, seeing language as a technique for crafting the piece of literature just as an artist crafts a piece of art like a sculpture or a painting

- Whereas Realism attempted to portray external objects and events as the common or middle class man sees them in everyday life, *impressionism* tries to portray the psychological impressions these objects and events make on characters, emphasizing the role of individual perception and exploring the nature of the conscious and unconscious mind.

- Whereas Realism tried to focus on these external objects and events, *expressionism* tried to express the inner vision, the inner emotion, or the inner spiritual reality that seem more important than the external realities of objects and events.

- Whereas Realism focused on external objects and events as they are (verisimilitude), *surrealism* tried to liberate the subconscious, to see connections overlooked by the logical mind, to deny the supreme authority of rationality and so portray objects and events as they *seem* rather than as they *are*.

○ Whereas Realism tried to show the supreme importance of 'rationalness' and reason, *absurdism* tried to duplicate in literature the absurd conditions of contemporary life: nameless millions dying in wars, commonplace horrors such as the Holocaust, a world in which "God is dead" cast mankind afloat in a chartless and unknowable world void of a spiritual center, the ultimate absurd circumstances in which contemporary humankind found itself.

8. Symbolism

Symbolism refers to the European cultural movement that was at its peak in the last two decades of the 19th century, profoundly affecting the visual arts and closely bound up with music and literature.

Symbolism was first identified as a literary movement in France (1856-1910), its basics were stated in the Symbolist Manifesto (1886). Its complex aesthetic was a mix of Platonic-inspired philosophy, mystical and occult doctrines, psychology, linguistics, science, political theory and such aesthetic issues as the relationship between abstraction and representation. While many Symbolists reacted against the materialism of 19th-century science and its implications, others sought to reconcile modern science with spiritual traditions. Ideas based on the rise of scientific psychology with its emphasis on individual freedom and the great interest in the occult, together with such practices as hypnosis, opened up a realm of psychic experience, which promised access to important realms of knowledge. Symbolism stressed feeling and evocation over definition and fact and emphasized the power of suggestion. Stephane Mallarmé wrote in 1891, 'To *name* an object is to suppress three-fourths of the enjoyment of the poem that comes from the delight of divining little by little; to *suggest* it, there is the dream.' It was felt that empirical science left no room for the spirit; however, psychological theory and occult doctrines explained perception and cognition as symbolic processes and indicated a spiritual path to understanding. These spiritual insights were obtained via intuition, fantasy, imagination and such subjective and irrational experiences as dreams, visions, hypnotism and alchemy. Baudelaire's lines from his poem *Correspondance* (1857), which have the roots of symbolism in them, illustrate the belief in the connection between nature and the soul: 'Nature is a temple of living pillars/where often words emerge, confused and dim;/and man goes through this forest, with/familiar eyes of symbols always watching him.'

Symbolism was largely a reaction against naturalism and realism, anti-idealistic movements which attempted to capture reality in its gritty particularity, and to elevate the humble and the ordinary over the ideal. These movements invited a reaction in favour of spirituality, the imagination, and dreams; the path to symbolism began with that reaction. Symbolist poetry emphasized non-structured "internalized" poetry that, for lack of better words, describe thoughts and feelings in disconnected ways and places logic, formal structure, and descriptive reality in the back seat. Influences on the Symbolist poets included the dark, introspective romanticism of William Blake and Edgar Allan Poe. Charles Baudelaire is often perceived as the foremost precursor of Symbolist poetry. Symbolist poetry influenced the 20th century "modernist" poets such as Ezra Pound and T. S. Eliot, as well as the movements of French Surrealism and Imagism. Both Yeats and Eliot were profoundly influenced by Arthur Symons' famous book *The Symbolist Movement in Literature*, which introduced the French Symbolist Poetry to the modernist British poets.

(10) Allegory and Personification

Allegory is a work of written, oral, or visual expression that uses symbolic figures, objects, and actions to convey truths or generalizations about human conduct or experience. It encompasses such forms as the fable and parable. Characters often personify abstract concepts or types, and the action of the narrative usually stands for something not explicitly stated. Symbolic allegories, in which characters may also have an identity apart from the message they convey, have frequently been used to represent political and historical situations and have long been popular as vehicles for satire. Edmund Spenser's long poem *The Faerie Queen* is a famous example of a symbolic allegory.

Allegory is a narration or description usually restricted to a single meaning because its events, actions, characters, settings, and objects represent specific abstractions or ideas. Although the elements in an allegory may be interesting in themselves, the emphasis tends to be on what they ultimately mean. Characters may be given names such as Hope, Pride, Youth, and Charity; they have few if any personal qualities beyond their abstract meanings. These personifications are not symbols because, for instance, the meaning of a character named Charity is precisely that virtue.

Generally, allegory is a story illustrating an idea or a moral principle in which objects take on symbolic meanings. In Dante's *Divine Comedy*, Dante, symbolizing humankind, is taken by Virgil the poet on a journey through Hell, Purgatory and Paradise in order to teach him the nature of sin and its punishments, and the way to salvation.

Let us define allegory: It is a story in which things and people represent something entirely other, perhaps an idea or a philosophy. Allegories typically contain within a moral or lesson. Let us refer to an example: George Orwell's *Animal Farm* is an allegorical tale in which farm animals represent Communist Russia. The pigs symbolize the government; the dogs are the police force; and the rest of the animals symbolize the working class

Allegory (from Greek: *allos*, "other", and *agoreuein*, "to speak") is a figurative mode of representation conveying a meaning other than the literal. Allegory teaches a lesson through symbolism. Allegory communicates its message by means of symbolic figures, actions or symbolic representation. Allegory need not be necessarily be expressed in language: it may be addressed to the eye, and is often found in realistic painting, sculpture or some other form of mimetic or representative art. Thus an allegory is a device that can be presented in literary form, such as a poem or novel, or in visual form, such as in painting or sculpture. As a literary device, an allegory in its most general sense is an extended metaphor. As an artistic device, an allegory is a visual symbolic representation. An example of a simple visual allegory is the image of the 'grim reaper'. Viewers understand that the image of the grim reaper is a symbolic representation of death. However, images and fictions with several possible interpretations are not allegories in the true sense. It may be noted that not every fiction with general application is an allegory.

Allegory and its relation to (1) Metaphor, (2) Parable and (3) Personification:

Let us refer to the relationship allegory has with other figures of speech. Allegory is a form of extended metaphor, in which objects, persons, and actions in a narrative, are equated with the meanings that lie outside the narrative itself. The underlying meaning has moral, social, religious, or political significance, and characters are often personification of abstract ideas as charity, greed, or envy. Thus an allegory is a story with two meanings, a literal meaning and a symbolic meaning.

A writer sometimes extends a metaphor through a long narrative so that objects, persons, and actions in the text are equated with meanings that lie outside the text. The most famous allegory in English is John Bunyan's *Pilgrim's Progress* (1678), a tale of Christian salvation.

Sometimes allegory takes the form of parable, particularly in poetry. Parable in poetry could be the form of a narrative or story that has a second meaning beneath the surface one. For example, Robert Frost is notable for his use of the parable using the description to evoke an idea. Some critics call him a "Parablist." Frost's poem "After Apple Picking" suggests the idea of apple harvest as accomplishment. His famous poem "Birches" suggests the value of learning and experience.

Allegory is a story or visual image with a second distinct meaning partially hidden behind its literal or visible meaning. The principal technique of allegory is personification, whereby abstract qualities are given human shape- as in public statues of Liberty or Justice. An allegory may be conceived as a metaphor that is extended into a structured system. In written narrative, allegory involves a continuous parallel between two (or more) levels of meaning in a story, so that its persons and events correspond to their equivalents in a system of ideas or a chain of events external to the tale: each character and episode in John Bunyan's *The Pilgrim's Progress*, for example, embodies an idea within a preexisting Puritan doctrine of salvation. Allegorical thinking permeated the Christian literature of the Middle Ages, flourishing in the morality plays and in the dream visions of Dante and Langland. Some later allegorists like Dryden and Orwell used allegory as a method of satire; their hidden meanings are political rather than religious.

Personification

Personification is a figure of speech in which inanimate objects or abstract ideas are endowed with human qualities, e.g., allegorical morality plays where characters include Good Deeds, Beauty, and Death. Another example: *Hunger sat shivering on the road* or *Flowers danced about the lawn.*

Personification is common in poetry wherein human characteristics are attributed to an abstract quality, animal, or inanimate object. Consider the following lines from Carl Sandburg's *Chicago*:

Stormy, husky, brawling,
City of the big shoulders.

Carl Sandburg description of Chicago includes shoulders. Cities do not have shoulders - people do. Sandburg personifies the city by ascribing to it something human - "shoulders." "Justice is blind" is another example.

Look at the following: "The Moon doth with delight / Look round her when the heavens are bare." (William Wordsworth, "Ode: Intimations of Immortality from Recollections of Early Childhood,") Another is "Death lays his icy hand on kings"(James Shirley, "The Glories of Our Blood and State,"). Personification has been used in European poetry since Homer and is particularly common in allegory; for example, the medieval morality play "Everyman" (c. 1500) and the Christian prose allegory *Pilgrim's Progress* (1678) by John Bunyan contain characters such as Death, Fellowship, Knowledge, Giant Despair, Sloth, Hypocrisy, and Piety. Personification became almost an automatic mannerism in 18th-century Neoclassical poetry, as exemplified by these lines from Thomas Gray's "An Elegy Written in a Country Church Yard": Here rests his head upon the lap of earth/ A youth to Fortune and to Fame unknown:/Fair science frowned not on his humble birth,/ And Melancholy marked him for her own. John Ruskin termed sentimentalized, exaggerated personification the "pathetic fallacy."

(11) Asides, Soliloquies

An Aside refers to a few words or a short passage in drama spoken by one character to the audience while the other actors on stage pretend that they cannot hear the speaker's words. It is a theatrical convention that the aside is not audible to other characters on stage. An aside is directed to the audience that supposedly is not audible to the other characters onstage at the time. When Hamlet first appears onstage, for example, his aside "A little more than kin, and less than kind!" gives the audience a strong sense of his alienation from King Claudius.

Contrast with soliloquy. The aside is usually indicated by stage directions.

A Soliloquy is a monologue spoken by an actor at a point in the play when the character believes that he/she is alone. The technique frequently reveals a character's innermost thoughts, including his feelings, state of mind, motives or intentions. The soliloquy often provides necessary but otherwise inaccessible information to the audience. The dramatic convention is that whatever a character says in a soliloquy to the audience must be true, or at least true in the eyes of the character speaking (i.e. whatever he states in a soliloquy is a true reflection of what the speaker believes or feels). The soliloquy was rare in Classical drama, but Elizabethan and Jacobean playwrights used it extensively, especially for their villains. Playwrights use soliloquies as a convenient way to inform the audience about a character's motivations and state of mind. Shakespeare's Hamlet delivers perhaps the best known of all soliloquies, which begins: "To be or not to be." Other well-known examples include speeches by the title characters of *Macbeth, Richard III,* and also Iago in *Othello.* Unlike the aside, a soliloquy is not usually indicated by specific stage directions.

Soliloquies and asides

Whereas a soliloquy is like a thought that the actors say out loud, an aside is directed at the audience, for example, in *The Country Wife*, where actors often focus on just a small group of people and make fun of the other characters on stage. Let us note the difference carefully : a soliloquy is a speech you make to yourself. A dramatic monologue is a speech made by yourself to a silent audience. An aside is a line spoken by yourself that is intended for the audience to hear but not the other people on stage. In all of these examples, the 'you' is referring to an actor in a play. So the difference is in who is intended to hear the speech and how long it is - an aside has the same audience as a monologue but is a very brief, quick line.

A soliloquy should also be distinguished from a "dramatic aside", which is a comment spoken during a passage of dialogue, though not meant to be heard by the other characters. It usually comments on, or contrasts with, the dialogue it accompanies. For example, Shylock's lengthy aside beginning *Yes, to smell pork* (Act 1, Scene iii) is obviously directed at Bassanio, though he is not intended to hear it, and is slotted into the dialogue of the scene. It is also part of the time-scheme of the dialogue; there is often a feeling in soliloquy that a character has stepped "outside time" to reflect, whereas Shylock's comments occupy a brief and specific moment in the dialogue.

(12) Comic Relief

Comic relief in serious plays or tragedies serves the artistic function of relieving the minds of the audience. Therefore it usually means a release of emotional or other tension resulting from a comic episode interposed in the midst of serious or tragic elements in a drama. It is a humorous scene, incident, character, or bit of dialogue occurring after some serious or tragic moment. Comic relief is deliberately designed to relieve emotional intensity and simultaneously heighten and highlight the seriousness or tragedy of the action. Such a humorous scene or incident alleviates tension in an otherwise serious work. In many instances these moments enhance the thematic significance of the story in addition to providing laughter. *Macbeth* contains Shakespeare's most famous example of comic relief in the form of a drunken porter. When Hamlet jokes with the gravediggers we laugh, but something hauntingly serious about the humor also intensifies our more serious emotions. The Gravedigger's scene is one of the best examples of comic relief. In addition to offering relief, it also indirectly underlines the theme of the play.

Sometimes comic relief characters will appear in fiction that is comic. This generally occurs when the work enters a dramatic moment, but the character continues to be comical regardless. Greek tragedy does not allow any comic relief. Even the Elizabethan critic Sidney following Horace's *Ars Poetica* pleaded for the exclusion of comic elements from a tragic drama. But in the Renaissance England, Marlowe among the University Wits introduced comic relief through the presentation of crude scenes in *Doctor Faustus* following the native tradition of Interlude which was usually introduced between two tragic plays. In fact, in the classical tradition the mingling of the tragic and the comic was not allowed.

Shakespeare deviated from the classical tradition and used comic relief in Hamlet, Macbeth, Othello and Romeo and Juliet. The mockery of the fool in *King Lear* may also be regarded as a comic relief. This tradition of comic relief in serious plays continues from the Mystery and Morality plays of the Medieval England. The comic talk in *Crucifixion* and slapping of Noah's wife in *Noah's Arc* are crude examples of comic relief.

(13) Poetic Justice

Poetic justice is a literary device in which virtue is ultimately rewarded or vice punished, often in modern literature by an ironic twist of fate intimately related to the character's own conduct.

Poetic justice refers to the morally reassuring allocation of happy and unhappy fates to the virtuous and the vicious characters respectively, usually at the end of a narrative or dramatic work. The term was coined by the critic Thomas Rymer in his *The Tragedies of the Last Age Consider'd* (1678) with reference to Elizabethan poetic drama. He used it to describe how a work should inspire proper moral behaviour in its audience by illustrating the triumph of good over evil He claimed that a narrative or drama should distribute rewards and punishments proportionately to the virtues and villainies of each character in the story. Thus, when a particularly vicious character meets a despicable end appropriate for his crimes, we say it is "poetic justice." Philip Sidney, in *Defense of Poetry,* argued that poetic justice was, in fact, the reason that fiction should be allowed in a civilized nation.

Poetic justice occurs more often in the fictional plots of plays than in real life. As Miss Prism explains in Oscar Wilde's *The Importance of Being Earnest*, 'The good ended happily, and the bad unhappily. That is what Fiction means.' In a slightly different but commonly used sense, the term may also refer to a strikingly appropriate reward or punishment, usually a 'fitting retribution' by which a villain is ruined by some process of his own making. However, this formula for resolving plots has fallen into disfavor in later centuries, and widely influential critics today don't advocate such a formula without qualifications.

The term is sometimes used with an ironic overtone. Poetic justice is when a reward or punishment occurs in a fitting matter, which often happens in works of fiction. This is often ironic. For example, if a poor man who was poor because he donated every cent to charity won the lottery, it would be poetic justice. If a thief who never got caught finally went to jail for a crime he never committed, it would be poetic justice and also ironic.

(14) The Intentional Fallacy

Literary criticism which takes account of authorial intention in a work in order to interpret it is supposed to commit an error or a fallacy called *the intentional fallacy.*

The intentional fallacy "is a confusion between the poem and its origins;" it begins by trying to derive the standard of criticism from the psychological *causes* of the poem and ends in biography and relativism. The phrase was first used by New Critics.

Intentional fallacy, in literary criticism, addresses the assumption that the meaning intended by the author of a literary work is of primary importance. By characterizing this assumption as a "fallacy," a critic suggests that the author's intention is not important. The term is an important principle of New Criticism and was first used by Wimsatt and Beardsley in their essay "The Intentional Fallacy" (1946): "the design or intention of the author is neither available nor desirable as a standard for judging the success of a work of literary art." The phrase "intentional fallacy" is somewhat ambiguous, but it means "a fallacy about "intent" and not "a fallacy committed on purpose."

Wimsatt and Beardsley in the famous 1946 essay divide the evidence used in making interpretations of literary texts into three categories:

(1) Internal evidence. This evidence is present as the facts of a given work. The apparent content of a work is the internal evidence, including any historical knowledge which we can notice in it. This internal evidence is discovered through the semantics and syntax of a poem, through our habitual knowledge of the language, through grammars, dictionaries, and all the literature which is the source of dictionaries, in general through all that makes a language and culture. Wimsatt has no objection to using this evidence for interpretation of a literary work.

(2) External evidence. What is not actually contained in the work itself is external. It includes statements made privately or published in journals about the work, or in conversations etc. External evidence is concerned with claims about why the artist made the work: reasons external to the fact of the work in itself. Evidence of this type is directly concerned with what the artist may have intended to do even or especially when it is not apparent from the work itself. This is external to the work; it is private or idiosyncratic, not part of the work as a linguistic fact: it consists of revelations about how or why the poet wrote the poem. Wimsatt objects to this sort of evidence if it is used for interpreting a work of art.

(3) Contextual evidence. The third kind of evidence concerns any meanings derived from the specific work's relationship to other art made by the same artist. It can be biographical, but does not necessarily mean it is a matter of intentional fallacy. This refers to private or semiprivate meanings attached to words or topics by an author. It is not easy to accept or reject this evidence. I this type (3) is closer to type (1), it may be accepted. But if (3) is closer to (2), it should be treated as external to the work and should be rejected. Or else in criticism it would amount to committing Intentional Fallacy.

Thus, a text's internal evidence - the words themselves, and their meanings - is fair game for literary analysis. External evidence - anything not contained within the text itself, such as information about the poet's life - belongs to literary biography, not literary criticism. Preoccupation with the author "leads away from the poem." According to New Criticism, a poem does not belong to its author, but rather "it is detached from the author at birth and goes about the world beyond his power to control it. The poem belongs to the public." It is the *Contextual evidence* that presents the greatest potential for intentional fallacies of interpretation. Analysis using this type of evidence can easily become more concerned with external evidence than the internal content of the work.

Intentional fallacy is committed because of the widespread assumption that an author's declared or supposed intention in writing a work is the proper basis for deciding on the meaning and the value of that work. Therefore, the New Critics argue that a literary work, once published, belongs in the public realm of language, which gives it an objective existence distinct from the author's original idea of it: 'The poem is not the critic's own and not the author's (it is detached from the author at its birth and goes about the world beyond his power to intend about it or control it). The poem belongs to the public.' Thus any information we may have about the author's intention cannot in itself determine the work's meaning or value, since it still has to be verified against the work itself. Many other critics have pointed to the unreliability of authors as witnesses to the meanings of their own works, which often have significances wider than their intentions in composing them. For example D. H. Lawrence once wrote, 'Never trust the artist. Trust the tale.'

If a statement made by the author is available and we have access to it, we should treat it only as an act of self-interpretation by the author,

While New Critics do not deny the presence of an authorial intention, they deny the importance or usefulness of looking for such an intention as part of analyzing a work. "To insist on the designing intellect as a *cause* of a poem is not to grant the design or intention as a *standard* by which the critic is to judge the worth of the poet's performance." Wimsatt and Beardsley argue that the poem must work on its own, independent of any meeting or not meeting of an authorial intention which a reader would have no immediate way of knowing about in the first place.

(15) Round and Flat Characters

The distinction between two types of characters- round and flat- has now become conventional and stereotypical. A round character is one who is multidimensional, revealing the complexity and contradictions that are so much a part of human nature. E.M. Forster, who first used the phrase in *Aspects of the Novel*, wrote that the true test of roundness is in a character's ability to surprise in a convincing way. The round character stands in contrast to the flat character, a term also coined by Forster. Flat characters tend to be defined by a single trait. They usually remain unchanged.

One can define Flat characters as minor characters in a work of fiction who do not undergo substantial change or growth in the course of a story. Also referred to as single dimensional characters or static characters, they play a supporting role to the main character, who as a rule should be round.

A flat char would be rather one dimentional, whereas a round character would be one who has many traits. Usually a novel might have a round character as its central protagonist, whereas other characters might be flat. A static character would stay the same throughout the story, and a dynamic character would change. Coming of age books, such as *To Kill a Mockingbird*, typically have at least one character who develops and changes as the story unfolds.

A round character is one with depth, faults, good points, complexity; this character is interesting and has an 'inner life'. A dynamic character is a character with energy and life and could also be one that changes during the course of the book. A dynamic character could drive the narrative and influence those around him/her. A dynamic character evolves through the course of the story or novel. A round character is fully developed so that the reader has a good picture of their looks and personality.

A static character stays the same, doesn't change during the course of the story. A flat character, or stock character, is like a filler - somebody who plays a role but has no personality that is pertinent to the story, like "storekeeper," or "police officer."

Though writers don't generally strive to write flat characters, they are often necessary in a story, along with round characters. Take, for example, Mr. Collins in *Pride and Prejudice*. He serves a vital role in the story of how Elizabeth and Darcy get together, and he provides comedy, but his character stays essentially unchanged. The origin of this concept of characterization is found in Ben Jonson's type of comedy named 'Comedy of Humours.' These plays abound in one-dimentional, flat characters. They were generally driven by one trait or humour. Although literature retains its great quality because of round characters like Hamlet and Macbeth, it also needs the common humanity which is full of flat characters.

□□

5
Practical Criticism

Practical criticism is a relatively young discipline. It began in the 1920s with a series of experiments by the Cambridge critic I.A. Richards. He gave poems to students without any information about who wrote them or when they were written. In *Practical Criticism* of 1929 he reported on and analysed the results of his experiments. The objective of his work was to encourage students to concentrate on 'the words on the page', rather than relying on preconceived or received beliefs about a text. For Richards this form of close analysis of anonymous poems was ultimately intended to have psychological benefits for the students: by responding to all the currents of emotion and meaning in the poems and passages of prose which they read, the students were to achieve what Richards called an 'organised response'. This meant that they would clarify the various currents of thought in the poem and achieve a corresponding clarification of their own emotions.

Later on Richards' most influential student, William Empson provided the basis for an entire critical method. In *Seven Types of Ambiguity* (1930) Empson developed complex and multiple meanings of poems. His work had a profound impact on a critical movement known as the New Criticism, the exponents of which tended to see poems as elaborate structures of complex meanings. New Critics would usually pay relatively little attention to the historical setting of the works which they analysed, treating literature as a sphere of activity of its own.

Practical criticism today is more usually treated as an ancillary skill rather than the foundation of a critical method. It is a part of many examinations in literature at almost all levels, and is used to test students' responsiveness to what they read, as well as their knowledge of verse forms and of the technical language for describing the way poems create their effects.

Practical criticism in this form has no necessary connection with any particular theoretical approach, and has shed the psychological theories which originally underpinned it. The discipline does, however, have some ground rules which affect how people who are trained in it will respond to literature. It might be seen as encouraging readings which concentrate on the form and meaning of particular works, rather than on larger theoretical questions. The process of reading a poem in clinical isolation from historical processes also can mean that literature is treated as a sphere of activity which is separate from economic or social conditions, or from the life of its author.

What is practical criticism?

"One of the things you will almost certainly have to do as a student of literature is 'practical criticism'. Practical criticism is that exercise in which you are given a poem, or a passage of prose you have not seen before and are asked to write a critical analysis of it. Usually you are not told who wrote the poem or passage, and usually, too, you are not given any indication of what you might look for or say. We can sum it up, then, as criticism based on close analysis of a text in isolation." This is taken from John Peck & Martin Coyle's book *Practical Criticism.*

The basic question is: How do we go about finding a way into a poem by finding a theme? The process of studying a poem can be divided into three main steps. Once you are familiar with these steps, try them with regard to an unseen poem. Practical criticism of a poem is a matter of self study.

1. Think about the text.

When you have finished reading a text, think about it and ask yourself what common experiences it is dealing with: is it about love, war, marriage or revenge? By thinking logically and positively, use this step to help you overcome the first problem, *I have read the text, now I should study it: how do I start?* This step helps you find a way into understanding the text.

2. Analyse the text.

Then identify words and phrases which led you to choose your theme. Now look at these closely analysing in detail to see exactly how they portray the theme you are studying. In this step your ideas become more precise and detailed because you concentrate on finding the complexity of different elements which make up the major theme you are interested in.

3. Relate the part you have studied to the text as a whole.

This will help you to work out how the part you have studied in detail fits into the text as a whole. Generally Practical Criticism exercises are given in a simple format. The unseen text is followed by questions which you have to answer. Therefore you should go back to the poem after reading the questions and read the poem again keeping the questions in mind. In a limited sense, your job is to understand the poem only in the context of the questions. When you write the answers, don't give unnecessary explanations. Try always to be brief.

Exercises

The poems given below are not commonly read poems. In that sense, they are truly 'unseen.' Therefore read the following poems and answer the questions given below in brief.

1

Flood Year

Walking up the driftwood beach at day's end
I saw it, thrust up out of a hillock of sand-
a frail, bleached clench of fingers dried by wind-
the dead child's hand.

And they are mourning there still, though I forget,
the year of flood, the scoured ruined land,
the herds gone down the current, the farms drowned,
and the child never found.

When I was there the thick hurling waters
had gone back to the river, the farms were almost drained.
Banished half-dead cattle searched the dunes; it rained;
river and sea met with a wild sound.

Oh with a wild sound water flung into air
where sea met river; all the country round
no heart was quiet. I walked on the driftwood sand
and saw the pale crab crouched, and came to a stand
thinking, A child's hand. The child's hand.

Questions:

1. Bring out the impact of the description of the dead child's hand in line no. three.
2. What is the significance of the crab in line no. 16.
3. Comment on the use of articles in the last line. What does it suggest?
4. Comment critically on the use of rhyme in the poem.
5. What is the speaker's attitude toward the dead child? Do you identify with the view?

2

Butterfly on Rock

The large yellow wings, black-fringed,
were motionless.

They say the soul of a dead person
will settle like that on the still face.

But I thought: the rock has borne this;
this butterfly is the rock's grace
it's most obstinate and secret desire
to be a thing alive made manifest.

Forgot were the two shattered porcupines
I had seen die in the black forest.
Pain is unreal; death, an illusion:
There is no death in all the land,
I heard my voice cry;
And brought my hand down on the butterfly
And felt the rock move beneath my hand.

Questions:

1. Explain the image used in the first four lines of the poem. Is it symbolic?
2. What is the central idea of the poem? Which line or lines indicate it?
3. What does the line no. 6 mean? What has it to do with the last line?
4. Why did the speaker forget the death of the two porcupines?
5. 'The poem looks like a sonnet but is not a sonnet.' Explain why?

3

Women

Women have no wilderness in them,
They are provident instead.
Content in the tight hot cell of their hearts
To eat dusty bread.
They do not see cattle cropping red winter grass
They do not hear
Snow water going down under culverts
Shallow and clear.
They wait, when they should turn to journeys,
They stiffen, when they should bend.
They use against themselves that benevolence
To which no man is friend.
They cannot think of so many crops to a field
Or of clean wood cleft by an axe.

Their love is an eager meaninglessness
Too tense, or too lax.
They hear in every whisper that speaks to them
A shout and a cry.
As like as not, when they take life over their door-sills
They should let it go by.

Questions:

1. How does the poem indicate the qualities women do have by referring to the ones they don't have?
2. Explain briefly what the poet says about women's love.
3. Bring out, with examples, the paradox in women's built-in character.
4. Comment on the phrase: 'as like as' in line No.19.
5. Who, according to you, is the poet: a man or a woman? Give reasons for your view.

4

One Art

The art of losing isn't hard to master;
so many things seem filled with the intent
to be lost that their loss is no disaster.

Lose something every day. Accept the fluster
of lost door keys, the hour badly spent.
The art of losing isn't hard to master.

Then practice losing farther, losing faster:
places, and names, and where it was you meant
to travel. None of these will bring disaster.

I lost my mother's watch. And look! My last, or
next-to-last, of three loved houses went.
The art of losing isn't hard to master.

I lost two cities, lovely ones. And, vaster,
some realms I owned, two rivers, a continent.
I miss them, but it wasn't a disaster.

—Even losing you (the joking voice, a gesture
I love) I shan't have lied. It's evident
the art of losing's not too hard to master
though it may look like (Write it!) like disaster.

Questions:
1. What is the poem about? State it briefly.
2. Show how the speaker's tone grows gradually serious as the poem moves forward.
3. How does the poem end? What does the last stanza suggest?
4. Comment on the use of rhyme and the rhyme-scheme.
5. Explain the meaningful possibilities of the line repeated in the poem.

5

Winding Up

I live on the water, alone.
Without wife and children.
I have circled every possibility to come to this:

a low house by grey water,
with windows always open
To the stale sea. We do not choose such things,

but we are what we have made.
We suffer, the years pass,
we shed freight but not our need

for encumbrances. Love is a stone
that settled on the sea-bed
under grey water. Now, I require nothing

from poetry but true feeling,
no pity, no fame, no healing. Silent wife,
we can sit watching grey water,

and in a life awash
with mediocrity and trash live rock-like.

I shall unlearn feeling,
unlearn my gift. That is greater
and harder than what passes there for life.

Questions:
1. How does the title of the poem reflect its theme?
2. Explain the significance of the 'stone' imagery.
3. Who do you think is the speaker of the poem?
   How do you know?
4. What does the speaker wish to 'unlearn'?
   Explain it in the context of the poem's ending.
5. Comment on the form of the poem. Does the poem look like prose cut into lines of unequal length?

6

The Mountain

My students look at me expectantly.
I explain to them that the life of art is a life
of endless labour. Their expressions
hardly change; they need to know
a little more about endless labour.
So I tell them the story of Sisyphus,
how he was doomed to push
a rock up a mountain, knowing nothing
Would come of this effort
But that he would repeat it
indefinitely. I tell them

There is joy in this, in the artist's life,
That one eludes
judgment, and as I speak
I am secretly pushing a rock myself,
slyly pushing it up the steep
face of a mountain. Why do I lie
to those children? They aren't listening,
they aren't deceived, their fingers
tapping at the wooden desks-
So I retract
the myth; I tell them it occurs
in hell, and that the artist lies
because he is obsessed with attainment,
that he perceives the summit
as that place where he will live forever,
a place about to be
transformed by his burden: with every breath,
I am standing at the top of the mountain.
Both my hands are free. And the rock has added
height to the mountain.

Questions:

1. Is the poem only about 'endless labour' of an artist? Explain briefly.

2. Comment on the use of the Myth of Sisyphus in the poem?

3. Bring out the paradox between the poet's views given in the first and the second part of the poem.

4. Explain the ending (last three lines) of the poem.

5. Comment on the title of the poem.

7

Piano

Softly, in the dusk, a woman is singing to me;
Taking me back down the vista of years, till I see

A child sitting under the piano, in the boom of
  the tingling stings
And presenting the small, poised feet of a mother
  who smiles as she sings.

In spite of myself, the insidious mastery of song
Betrays me back, till the heart of me weeps to belong
To the old Sunday evenings at home, with winter outside
And hymns in the cozy parlour, the tinkling piano our guide.

So now it is vain for the singer to burst into clamour
With the great black piano appassionato. The glamour
Of childish days is upon me, my manhood is cast
Down in the flood of remembrance, I weep like a child
    for the past.

Questions:

1. How does the poem bring out the poet's personal response to loss?
2. Comment on the artistic use of the progressive tense in Stanza One.
3. Why does the poet use an out of the way word: appassionato?
4. Show how the present and the past become one in "Piano."
5. Why does the poet say, "the insidious mastery of song/ <u>Betrays</u> me back"?

8

You Came with Shells

You came with shells. And left them: shells.
They lay beautifully on the table.
Now they lie on my desk peculiar
extraordinary under 60 watts.

This morning I disturb I destroy the window
(and its light) by moving my feet in the water. There.

It's gone.
Last night the moon ranged from the left
to the right side
of the windshield. Only white lines
on a road strike me as reasonable but
nevertheless and too often
we slow down for the fog.

I was going to say a natural environment
means this or
I was going to say we remain out of our
element or
sometimes you can get away completely
but the shells
will tell about the howling and the loss.

Questions:

1. Though Wordsworthian, this is a modern nature poem. Do you agree? Why?
2. Comment on the nature imagery in the second 'stanza' of the poem.
3. Bring out the relationship between the 'I' and 'You' of the poem.
4. Illustrate how the speaking voice dominates the structure and vocabulary of the poem.
5. What, according to you, do 'shells' stand for? Explain briefly.

□□

Reference Books

1. Abrams, M. H. - A Glossary of Literary Terms (7th Ed.)

2. Brooks and Wimsatt - A Short History of Literary Criticism

3. Eliot, T. S. - Tradition and the Individual Talent

4. Hudson, W. H. - Introduction to the Study of Literature

5. Monfries, Helen - Critical Appreciation

6. Schreiber - Introduction to Literary Criticism

7. Scot, Wilbur - Five Approaches to Literature

8. Scott - James - Making of Literature

9. Sethuraman - Practical Criticism

10. Thorat, Ashok and others (2001), A Spectrum of Literary Criticism (Frank Bros)

11. Worsfold, Basil - Judgement of Literature

□□